New Amazonia

New Amazonia

A Foretaste of the Future

Elizabeth Burgoyne Corbett

MINT EDITIONS

New Amazonia: A Foretaste of the Future was first published in 1889.

This edition published by Mint Editions 2021.

ISBN 9781513299471 | E-ISBN 9781513223933

Published by Mint Editions®

MINT
EDITIONS

minteditionbooks.com

Publishing Director: Jennifer Newens
Design & Production: Rachel Lopez Metzger
Project Manager: Micaela Clark
Typesetting: Westchester Publishing Services

Contents

Prologue 7

I 13

II 19

III 23

IV 27

V 31

VI 36

VII 42

VIII 47

IX 53

X 58

XI 64

XII 71

XIII 78

XIV 85

XV 93

XVI 100

XVII 108

PROLOGUE

I t is small wonder that the perusal of that hitherto, in my eyes, immaculate magazine, the *Nineteenth Century*, affords me less pleasure than usual. There may possibly be some articles in it both worth reading and worth remembering, but of these I am no longer conscious, for an overmastering rage fills my soul, to the exclusion of everything else.

One article stands out with such prominence beyond the rest that, to all intents and purposes, this number of the *Nineteenth Century* contains nothing else for me. Not that there is anything admirable in the said article. Far from it. I look upon it as the most despicable piece of treachery ever perpetrated towards woman by women.

Indeed, were it not that some of the perpetrators of this outrage on my sex are well-known writers and society leaders, I would doubt the authenticity of the signatures, and comfort my soul with the belief that the whole affair has been nothing but a hoax got up by timorous and jealous male bipeds, already living in fear of the revolution in social life which looms before us at no distant date.

As it is, I am able to avail myself of no such doubtful solace, and I can only feel mad, downright mad—no other word is strong enough—because I am not near enough to these traitors to their own sex to give them a *viva voce* specimen of my opinion of them, though I resolve mentally that they shall taste of my vengeance in the near future, if I can only devise some sure method of bringing this about.

But perhaps by this time some of my readers, who may not have seen or heard of the objectionable article in question, may be anxious to know what this tirade is all about.

I will tell them.

But I must first allude to the fact that my sex really consists of three great divisions. To the first, but not necessarily the superior division, belongs the class which prefers to be known as *ladies*.

Ladies, or rather the class to which they belong, are generally found to rest their claim to this distinction, if it be one, upon the fact that they are the wives or daughters of prominent or well-to-do members of the other sex.

They find themselves in comfortable circumstances. The money or distinction which may be at the command of their husbands or fathers enables them to pass the greater portion of their time in dressing, or in airing such charms as they may possess. They lead for the most part a frivolous life, and their greatest glory is the reflected lustre which shines upon them by virtue of the wealth or attainments of their husbands or other male connections.

It is always noticeable that the less brains and claim for distinction a lady possesses herself, and the less actual cause she has for self-glorification, the higher and the more arrogantly does she hold her head above her fellows, and the more prone is she to despise and depreciate every woman who recognises a nobler aim in life than that of populating the world with offspring as imbecile as herself.

Il va sans dire that there are thousands of ladies to whom the last remark is scarcely applicable. Gentle in manners, and yielding in disposition, they are perfectly satisfied with the existing order of things, and quite believe the doctrine that man in his arrogance has laid down, that he is the God-ordained lord of creation, and that implicit obedience to his whims and fancies is the first duty of woman.

They have all they feel necessary to their well being. They have husbands who regard them as so much personal property, and who treat them alternately as pets or slaves; their wants are liberally provided for without any anxiety on their part; they rather like the idea of having little or no work to do, and to their mind, independence is a dreadful bugbear, which every lady ought to shun as she would shun a mad dog or a leper.

They are not to blame, poor things, for they are what man and circumstances have made them, and their general amiability and vague notions of doing what they have been taught is right, at all costs, partly exonerates such of them as have been persuaded to sign the *Nineteenth Century* protest.

Although I am not disposed to regard *ladies* as the wisest and most immaculate members of my sex, I do not include in this category all those who would fain usurp the doubtful distinction of being regarded as such. For instance: a young friend of mine, on her marriage, found herself domiciled in a very pretty little house in the suburbs, her domestic staff being limited to one maid-of-all-work.

One day, while the latter was out upon an errand, a tremendous ring at the front-door bell put my friend all in a flutter. She had but recently returned from her honeymoon, and wished to receive callers with becoming dignity. She would have preferred the maid to open the door, and show the visitor into her tiny drawing room; but as the maid was not at home, there was nothing for it but to officiate as door-opener herself.

She need not have been alarmed, for the individual at the door proved to be a big, fat, dirty, perspiring female, with a large basket of crockery-ware, some of which she tried to persuade my friend to buy. Finding her efforts in this direction fruitless, she began to wonder if she had been forestalled, and somewhat surprised my little friend by the following query: "If ye plaze, mum, can ye tell me if there's been *another lady* hawking pots about here this afternoon?"

No; decidedly this individual's claim to be regarded as a lady was somewhat too pretentious, and it must be understood that when speaking of *ladies*, I draw the line at hawkers.

The second great division of the female sex is composed of *women*. These do not sigh for society cognomens such as are essential to the happiness of their less thoughtful sisters. They want something more substantial. Many of them find it necessary to earn their own livelihood. Others possess a sufficient percentage of this world's good things to enable them to banish all dread of poverty in their own lives. Others, and I am glad to say that this class is ever on the increase, prefer to work, simply because they prize independence above all things.

No one will venture to suggest that these women are selfish egotists, for their aims and ambitions embrace the welfare of half the human race at least, and, whatever may be the ultimate results of their gallant fight on behalf of "Woman's Rights," they will be only too thankful to see them enjoyed by every other woman on the face of the earth.

Widely different from these is the third division of the feminine genus *homo*. *Slaves* they are. Neither more nor less. When emancipation comes to them, it will not be as a result of their own endeavours, for custom, perverted education, physical weakness, and lack of energy all combine to keep them in the groove into which they have been mercilessly trodden for centuries.

Fortunately some of them go through life without feeling terribly discontented. Their wily subjugators, led by the priesthood, have for centuries played upon feminine superstition and credulity, until they have succeeded in making them believe that their physical weakness, with its natural concomitant evil, intellectual inferiority, is foreordained by an omniscient Being whom they are expected to gratefully adore because of His great justice and mercy.

Now and again some of these slaves rebel, and are punished for breaking laws made by men for the benefit of men. Sometimes we hear of some woman who, driven either by lack of education, or by circumstances, has committed some outrage upon society which calls for terrible punishment. Perhaps she has been unfaithful to a wicked incarnation of lust and cruelty, who has for years indulged in *liaisons* of which all the world has been cognisant. She has had to put up with incredible slights and indignities, but as her husband has been cunning enough to refrain from beating and starving her, the law, as made and administered by men, allows her no escape from her irksome marital bonds.

But let her become reckless, and find solace in another man's love, then she becomes a social pariah, against whom our canting hypocritical Pharisees hold up their hands in denunciatory horror, and from whom the husband speedily obtains a judicial separation, applauded by sympathising male humbugs, and consoled by the "damages," valued at £5,000 or so, which the court has ordered the co-respondent to pay as a solatium for his wounded *affections*. Said co-respondent will not be improved in morals by the skinning process he has undergone, but will turn his attentions in future to ladies who have no husbands to claim golden solatium for lacerated feelings.

Corrupt, Degraded, Rotten to the core is British Civilisation, and yet we find women, who ought to know better, actually pretending that they are perfectly contented with the existing order of things.

And that brings me back to the *raison d'être* of this story. The *Nineteenth Century Magazine* has been guilty of condoning, if not of instigating, an atrocity. It has published a rigmarole, signed by a great many *ladies*, to the effect that Woman's Suffrage is not wanted by *women*, and, indeed, would hardly be accepted if it were offered to them. The principal signatories are in comfortable circumstances; have no great cares upon their shoulders; they plume themselves upon occupying prominent positions in society; it is to their interest to uphold the political principles of the men whose privilege it is to support them; they do not see that life need be made any brighter for them, therefore they conspire to prevent every other woman from emerging from the ditch in which she grovels.

Of course the other woman may be ambitious, or industrious, or miserable, or oppressed; but that has nothing to do with the fine ladies, whose arguments are as feeble as their hearts are callous, and whose principles are as unjustifiable as their selfishness is reprehensible.

"We have all we want," say these fair philanthropists, "and we intend to use our best endeavours to make other women regard their circumstances in the same light. They must be taught to duly acknowledge the reverence they owe to MAN and GOD. If we cannot persuade them that things are as they ought to be, we will take effectual means to prevent their further progress towards the emancipation some of them are treasonably preaching. Their morals we will leave to the priesthood to coddle and terrorise, but we must make them understand that MAN always was, always must, and always will be, of paramount power and wisdom in this world. Woman was but made from the rib of a man, and ought to know from this fact alone that she can never be his equal," and so on *ad nauseum*.

It would be wonderful if I, being a *woman*, did not feel indignant when being confronted with these and similar *crushing* arguments, which, if not all aired in the *Nineteenth Century*, are quite as strong as any which the deluded signatories have to advance in support of the despicably unwomanly attitude they have adopted.

Only a rib, forsooth! How do they know that woman was made out of nothing better than a man's rib? We have only a man's word for that, and I have proved the falsity of so many manly utterances that I would like some scientific proof as to the truth or falsity of the spare-rib argument before I give it implicit credence.

Thank goodness, the *Fortnightly Review* comes to the rescue with a gallant counter-protest, signed by the cream of British WOMANHOOD, and I feel viciously glad that I have been privileged to add my name to the long list of those who are determined to stand up for justice to their sex, whether they may happen to feel the need of it in their own individual cases or not. I am also delighted to find an influential magazine, conducted by men, which chivalrously does battle on behalf of my sex.

"Good old *Fortnightly*," I apostrophise mentally. "Long life and prosperity be thine," and I am confidently able to predict that there will be a persistent and flourishing *Fortnightly Review* of all things British long after the *Nineteenth Century* has become a thing of the past.

But here my attention is directed to the fact that two women, who have always womanfully championed the cause of their sex, have written replies to the anti-woman suffrage article, and that, furthermore, the editor of the *Nineteenth Century* has inserted these replies in his review, which forthwith is absolved from a great share of the displeasure which the "atrocity" roused, not alone in my breast, but in thousands of other women—*and* MEN.

The last fact is justly emphasised in big letters, for it shows that at least some portion of the male sex recognises the enormity and injustice of saddling one-half of the human race with all the disabilities it is possible to heap upon it, except the disabilities of exemption from taxation and kindred methods of assisting in promoting the general welfare of the nation.

When I mention the fact that the two replies in the *Nineteenth* are written by Mrs. Fawcett and Mrs. Ashton Dilke respectively, I have, I think, given sufficient assurance that the replies are in themselves able ones.

Into such a good humour, in fact, have I been soothed by the perusal of the counter-protests, that I find myself stringing together all sorts of fancies in which women's achievements form conspicuous features, and I am just noticing how pleasant Mrs. Weldon looks in the Speaker's chair, listening to Mrs. Besant's first Prime Ministerial speech, when my senses become entirely "obfuscated," as Sambo would say, and I sink into slumber as profound as that which overcame the fabled enchanted guardians of my favourite enchanted palace.

I

The next event I can chronicle was opening my eyes on a scene at once so beautiful and strange that I started to my feet in amaze. This was not my study, and I beheld nothing of the magazine which was the last thing I remembered seeing before I went to sleep. I was in a glorious garden, gay with brilliant hued flowers, the fragrance of which filled the air with a subtle and delicate perfume; around me were trees laden with luscious fruits which I can only compare to apples, pears, and quinces, only they were as much finer than the fruits I had hitherto been familiar with as Ribstone pippins are to crabs, and as jargonelles are to greenbacks. Countless birds were singing overhead, and I was about to sink down again, and yield to a delicious languor which overpowered me, when I was recalled to the necessity of behaving more decorously by hearing someone near me exclaim in mystified accents, "By Jove! But isn't this extraordinary? I say, do you live here, or have you been taking hasheesh too?"

I looked up, and saw, perched on the limb of a great tree, a young man of about thirty years of age, who looked so ridiculously mystified at the elevated position in which he found himself, that I could not refrain from smiling, though I did not feel able to give an immediate satisfactory reply to his queries.

"Oh, that's right," he commented. "It makes a fellow relieved to see a smile, when he wasn't at all sure whether he wouldn't get sent to Jericho for perching up an apple tree. But really, I don't know how the deuce I came to be up here, that is, I beg your pardon, but I can't understand how I happen to be up this apple tree. And oh! by Jove! It isn't an apple tree, after all! Isn't it extraordinary?"

But I could positively do nothing but laugh at him for the space of a moment or two. Then I gravely remarked that as I supposed he was not glued to the tree, he had better come down, whereat he followed my advice, being unfortunate enough, however, to graze his hands, and tear the knees of his trousers during the process of disembarkation.

When at last he had relieved himself of a few spare expletives, delivered in a tone which he vainly flattered himself was too low for me to hear, he stood revealed before me, a perfect specimen of the British masher. His height was not too great, being, I subsequently ascertained five feet three, an inch less than my own, but he made the most of what there was of him by holding himself as erect as possible, and as he wore soles an inch thick to his otherwise smart boots, he looked rather taller than he really was.

His proportions were not at all bad, and I have seen a good many very much worse looking fellows who flattered themselves that they were quite killing. His face had lost the freshness of early youth, and looked as though it spent a great deal of its time in the haunts of dissipation. The moustache, however, was perfect—so golden, so long, so elegant was it, that it must have been the envy of countless members of the masher tribe, and I was not surprised to notice presently that its owner found his pet occupation in stroking it.

Just now, however, he was chiefly employed in lamenting the accident which had occurred to his nether garment, this being, by the way, one portion of a tweed suit of the most alarmingly demonstrative pattern and colour.

"By Jove!" he muttered, disconsolately, "it's awful! you know. When I was so careful, too! What on earth ever possessed me to mount that tree? Isn't it extraordinary?"

This time I was about to attempt a reply, when I was struck dumb with awe and astonishment, and my companion, who had found his own eyes sufficiently powerful to take in my appearance, hastily fixed a single eyeglass into position, and gazed in open-mouthed wonder at an apparition which approached us.

And he might well gaze, for of a surety the creature which we saw was something worth looking at, and a specimen of a race the like of which we had never seen before. "It is a woman," I thought. "A goddess!" the masher declared, and for a time I could not feel sure that he was mistaken.

She was close upon seven feet in height, I am sure, and was of magnificent build. A magnified Venus, a glorified Hebe, a smiling Juno, were here all united in one perfect human being whose gait was the very poetry of motion.

She wore a very peculiar dress, I thought, until I saw that science and common sense had united in forming a costume in which the requirements alike of health, comfort, and beauty had reached their acmé.

A modification of the divided skirt came a little below the knee, the stockings and laced boots serving to heighten, instead of to hide, their owner's beautiful symmetry of limb. A short skirt supplemented the graceful tunic, which was worn slightly open at the neck, and partially revealed the dainty whiteness of a shapely bust. The whole costume was of black velvet, and was set off by exquisite filmy laces, and by a crimson sash which confined the tunic at the waist, and hung gracefully on the left side of the wearer.

She was wearing a silver-embroidered velvet cap, which she courteously doffed on beholding us, and I noticed that her hair, but an inch or two long, curled about her head and temples in the most delightfully picturesque fashion imaginable.

She was surprised to see us, that was quite apparent, but she evidently mistook our identity for awhile. "What strange children!" she exclaimed, in a rich, sonorous voice, which was bewitchingly musical. "Why are you here, and for what particular purpose are you masquerading in this extraordinary fashion?"

"Yes, it is extraordinary, isn't it?" burst forth the masher, "but you are slightly mistaken about us. I can't answer for this lady, and I really don't know what the deuce she is doing here, but I am the Honourable Augustus Fitz-Musicus. I daresay you have heard of me. My ancestor, you know, was King George the Fourth. He fell in love with a very beautiful lady, who, until the first gentleman in Europe favoured her with his attentions, was an opera singer. She subsequently became the mother of a family, who were all provided for by their delighted father, the king. The eldest son was created Duke of Fitz-Musicus, and he and his family were endowed with a perpetual pension for 'distinguished services rendered to the State, you know.'"

"Then you are not a little boy?" queried the giantess. "But of course you must be. Come here, my little dear, and tell me who taught you to say those funny things, and who pasted that queer little moustache on your face."

As she spoke she actually stooped, kissed the Honourable Augustus Fitz-Musicus on the forehead, and patted him playfully on the cheek with one shapely finger. This was, however, an indignity not to be borne patiently, and the recipient of these well-meant attentions indignantly sprang on one side, his face scarlet, and his voice tremulous with humiliated wrath.

"How dare you?" he gasped. "How dare you insult me so? You must know that I am not a child. Your own hugeness need not prevent you from seeing that *I am a man*."

"A man! never! O, this is too splendid a joke to enjoy by myself." Saying this, and laughing until the tears came into her eyes, the goddess raised her voice a little, and called to some companions who were evidently close at hand, "Myra! Hilda! Agnes! oh, do come quickly. I have found two such curious creatures."

In response to this summons three more girls of gigantic stature came from the further end of the garden, and completed our discomfiture by joining in the laugh against us.

"What funny little things! Wherever did you find them, Dora?" queried one of the new comers, whereat Dora composed her risible faculties as well as she was able, and explained that she had just found us where we were, and that one of us claimed to be a *man*.

Myra and Agnes were quite as amused at this as Dora had been, but Hilda took the situation somewhat more seriously. She had noted how furious the Honourable Augustus Fitz-Musicus looked, and observed my vain attempt to assume a dignified demeanour in the presence of such a formidable array of playful goddesses, who now all plied us with questions together.

I did not feel much inclined to converse, for I was terribly afraid of being ridiculed. But Hilda questioned me so much more sensibly, in my opinion, than the others, that I was disposed to be more communicative to her than to them.

"Where do you come from?" she questioned gently, as if she were afraid of injuring me by using her normal voice.

"I am English," I replied proudly, feeling quite sure that the very name of my beloved native land would prove a talisman of value in any part of the globe. But although the beautiful quartette refrained from laughing, they listened to me in mystified astonishment, partly, I perceived, because my small voice was a revelation to them, and partly because my answer conveyed no understandable meaning to them.

"English," at last said Agnes. "What do you mean by English? There is no such nation now. I believe that centuries ago Teuto-Scotland used to be called England, and that it used to be inhabited by the English, a warlike race which is now extinct."

"My dear Agnes," interposed Hilda, "You surely forget that we are ourselves descended from this great race. But suppose we go on with our questions. Not so fast my little man; here, I will take care of you for the present."

The last exclamation was evoked by an attempt on the part of the Honourable Augustus to escape while the attention of the party was concentrated upon myself. He was, however, foiled in his attempt, and

Hilda coolly seated him upon a tall garden seat, as if he were a baby, and kept a detaining hand on his wrist, while she listened to the replies I now made to my tormentors. "What is your name?" was the next interrogatory to which I was subjected. I did not consider it necessary to go into details, so merely gave my name. Other questions were now asked me, but I was so determined to give no food for ridicule, if I could help it, that I was rather obstinate in refusing information, and at last took refuge in the remark, delivered as quietly as my tingling nerves would permit, "That in my country people were polite to strangers, and did not interrogate them as if they were so many wild beasts."

Even while giving utterance to this remark, I remembered several scenes which proved that it was far from true. But the goddesses did not know this much, and my reproof served to convince them that the Honourable Augustus and myself were not monkeys that had learnt the art of speech, and been dressed for exhibition, but actual, though very queer, specimens of the human race divine.

Apologies for their rudeness were now freely tendered by the giantesses, and one of them proposed to take us into the house at once and supply us with refreshments. No sooner said than done, and I hardly know whether I was most amused or humiliated to find myself led by the hand, as if I were only just learning to walk, and must be carefully guarded from stumbling.

It was some consolation to observe that the Honourable Augustus was served likewise, and that he was lifted up the huge steps which must be ascended to enter the house just as easily as I was. We were taken into a large hall, which seemingly served as a refectory, for I observed a table in the centre, upon which many covers were laid.

Just at this juncture a great bell was rung somewhere in the building, and about fifty other individuals entered the room, but crowded round us instead of round the table, as was evidently their first intention. They were, however, upon the whole, quite as polite as a room full of English people would be, were our respective positions reversed, and Hilda constituted herself our protector from bothering questions until dinner was served. The seats and table were on a somewhat larger scale than I had been hitherto used to, but a cushion considerately brought for me made me comfortable enough.

While being quizzed by such a number of eyes, I diligently used my own, and noted that all these magnificent creatures, except six, were apparently young students, and that they were all habited in somewhat similar fashion to Dora, such difference as there was consisting, not in shape or cut, but in variety of material and colouring.

The six exceptions were perfectly beautiful women, all approaching middle age, and with less exuberance of spirit, but more dignity of manner than the others. Their dress also was slightly different, their tunics being ornamented with rich facings, and their sashes, worn on the right side, being composed of a gorgeous material something like cloth of gold, but so soft in texture as to drape gracefully.

A number of attendants served the meal, and these were all attired in the national garb, with the exception of the sashes, while their clothes were, for the most part, composed of washing materials, in which they looked very pictures of neatness and cleanliness.

As soon as the meal had begun, we were less scrutinised than we had been, and I now discovered myself to be very hungry, and disposed to do full justice to the appetising viands set before me. There was a variety of dainty dishes to choose from, and much fruit, all of which was marvellously sweet and luscious. But there was no dish that I could see prepared from animal food, and I resolved to discover later whether such a strange omission was of regular or only occasional occurrence.

II

After dinner was over the students indulged in conversation. I discovered afterwards that music usually formed a prominent feature in after dinner amusements, but today the Honourable Augustus and myself afforded sufficient food for pastime. We were, however, not exactly mobbed, though our audience was a large one in every sense of the word. One thing puzzled me exceedingly. When I spoke awhile ago of being "English," my interrogators seemed thoroughly mystified, and yet they were speaking my native tongue in all its insular purity. Evidently there was a good deal to explain on all sides.

Augustus Fitz-Musicus had by this time got over his chagrin, and was, I could tell, even congratulating himself in a mild sort of way over the fact that he was proving a much greater source of attraction than I was. He was receiving the attentions of this bevy of big beauties with such a ridiculous air of conceited nonchalance, that I was provoked to laughter, in spite of my polite attempt to restrain my mirth.

Myra comprehended the cause of my amusement, and whispered, "I see, little lady, that the male biped is the same all the world over,—a conglomeration of conceit and arrogance. Your little man looks too funny for anything, and yet I will warrant that he thinks himself capable of captivating one half of us. What is he thought of in your country?"

But to this question I was unable to give a satisfactory answer, as I could only say that I was perfectly ignorant of everything connected with the Honourable Augustus, never having seen him in my life until today.

This reply amazed Myra and others who heard it, but further interrogations on her part were stopped for a little while by the advent of the Lady Principal and two of the professors, who wished to speak with me and to know how I came to be here.

The young students respectfully made way for them, and I confess that my sensations on beholding them approached something very near akin to awe. The Lady Principal, especially, was a being to be remembered. In height she was somewhat superior to the others. Her features were so perfect in outline and expression that I think Minerva must have looked like this woman did. There was not one among all these women who did not look the embodiment of health. Principal Helen Grey did more than this; she seemed to me to be the goddess of health herself, and to be capable of endowing others with this most to be prized earthly blessing.

She sat down beside me, and gently asked me who I was, and how I happened to be here. My answer to the effect that I did not know how I had got here was evidently a tax on her credulity, but she was too well bred to do aught but listen quietly while I continued my explanations.

I told of my perusal of certain magazines, and how my feelings had been strongly excited upon one subject, until I must have gone to sleep while thinking of it. Then I described my awaking amid strange surroundings, and that I supposed the Honourable Fitz-Musicus had been transported hither also. My account of our first interview with each other provoked amusement, and every face around me rippled with smiles.

After a few moment's musing, Principal Grey asked me what I meant by saying that a certain article deprecated the introduction of Women's Suffrage into my country. "Do you mean to say," she asked, "that men are the only voters in your country?"

"Yes," I replied, "and men are not the only obstacle to woman's advancement in England. Only a small minority of women dare avow their real opinions on this very subject. More stupid and less enlightened females hurl all sorts of contemptible reproaches at them for presuming to endeavour to better the condition of their sex. All the laws of my country have been made by men, and they are all made in the interests of men. It is only a few years since it was possible for a married woman to hold property in her own right. She might earn, or in any other way acquire, a large fortune. Her husband could take and squander every penny of it, without the least fear of being taxed with having done more than he had a perfect right to do." "Your England, as you call it, must be a strange country," said Principal Grey. "But I cannot quite make out where it is. I am not considered ignorant in matters appertaining to history and geography, but I am unable to locate this England of yours. Once upon a time, a matter of a thousand years ago, the neighbouring island, which is now called Teuto-Scotland, was called Albion, and later on England, but we have always understood ourselves to be the only race living which is at all representative of England and the ancient English."

"And what country is this?" I enquired in my turn, marvelling much to hear this giantess speak of "the ancient English."

"This country is New Amazonia. A long time ago it was called Erin by some, but Ireland was the name it was best known by. It used to be the scene of perpetual strife and warfare. Our archives tell us that it was

ELIZABETH BURGOYNE CORBETT

subjugated by the warlike English, and that it suffered for centuries from want and oppression. The land was appropriated by English mercenaries, who exacted enormous rents, which they spent anywhere but in Ireland. Famines, attempted revolutions and conspiracies, unjust repressive laws, and all sorts of calamities are said to have ruined and depopulated the country until the wars arose which resulted in our coming here. But as all is so strange here to you, you shall, if you care about it, be taken out this evening, and then you will be better able to judge what sort of people we are. Meanwhile, our duties must be attended to. Hilda, be good enough to take this woman to your room, until we can make other arrangements, and—oh dear, there is the little gentleman! What shall we do with him?"

The Honourable Augustus was being conducted through the principal reception rooms of the college, for such the building was, and the question of his ultimate disposal could be discussed without the embarrassment which his presence might perhaps have entailed.

"Suppose we request Mr. Medlock to take him until he decides what his future arrangements will be?" suggested Professor Wise, a lady who had hitherto taken no part in the conversation. "It would never do to let him sleep in the college for a night! The poor little thing's character would be irretrievably compromised."

"Of course it would," agreed Principal Grey, and she set about making the necessary arrangements forthwith, while I, wondering if I had been asleep for five or six centuries, followed Hilda to the upper story in which her sleeping room was situated. But long before I reached it I felt tired to death. The marble stairs were exceedingly massive, and were apparently interminable, while the beautiful banister rails were too large for me to grasp them with my hand, and thus help myself up. I was at last compelled to sit down exhausted, feeling that not one more step could I mount.

Hilda looked at me in astonishment, as I sat panting with my unwonted exertions. "Is it possible," she cried, "that the walk up these few steps has exhausted you? You must be ill, or is it the fault of the queer clothes that you wear that you are incapable of taking exercise? But whichever way it is, you cannot sit here, so be kind enough to excuse me."

The next moment I was lifted up as if I were a child, and Hilda ran nimbly up another long flight of steps with me, finally depositing me in a room that was very handsomely furnished, though most of the articles in it were of a style the like whereof I had never seen before. Seeing that

I had apparently been Rip-van-Winkelized for about six hundred years, this is not at all surprising.

But I could not help noticing a piano, which was the facsimile of one which was in my own possession before I fell asleep. In fact, I had an idea that it was the very same piano, though how it got here I could not imagine. Hilda saw me looking at it, and did not remove my mystification by remarking, "Yes, it is a curious old thing, isn't it, and in excellent preservation, I believe. We have several more of them in the capital, all formerly owned by Englishwomen who originally settled in Dublin after the wars."

"Then is this Dublin?" I asked. "If so, I am not so very far from home, after all."

"This place used to be called Dublin in the time of the ancient Irish, but when the country was turned over to what was then contemptuously called 'petticoat government,' nearly all place-names were changed, and the names of famous women applied to them. Thus we have Fawcetville, Beecherstown, Weldonia, Besantsville, Jarrettburn, and hundreds of other names, the etymological origin of which is easily traceable. In fact, it is one of our laws that no town or village shall receive a name which does not commemorate some woman who has done all she could to advance the interests of her sex."

Our conversation lasted awhile longer, but Hilda had her studies to attend to, and after reaching several books from a bookshelf for me to amuse myself with during her absence, she left me for awhile to my own devices promising to do all she could to make my visit a pleasant one.

There were many things here to arouse my curiosity, but I was most anxious to see if the books were printed in a style which I could understand, as I hoped to gain a great deal of information relative to the strange land in which I found myself, through no effort of will on my own part.

Fortunately I found the type and paper very beautiful, and with the exception that the spelling was considerably more phonetic than that in vogue with us, I found very little difference between our language as at present printed, and as exponed in the pages of "The History of Amazonia," which was the first book I opened.

I must have spent at least two hours in close reading, and if anyone would like to know the results of my investigations in posthumous history, she or he will find them recorded in the next chapter.

III

The history began with a brief resumé of such events as school books had long ago made me tolerably familiar with, but went on to say that it was in the reign of Victoria that the incidents which ultimately resulted in the disruption of the British Empire took place, though the final decisive steps did not eventuate until towards the close of the reign of her successor, who used his utmost endeavours to secure justice for all his subjects. But the factious discontent had been growing for so many years, that it was impossible for him, when he did at last come into power, to retrieve all the errors, and undo all the mischief, which had been done during the reign of his predecessor.

Ireland especially was troublesome, for it had always been made to feel that it was a subjugated State. The Sovereign sedulously petted and spoiled the northern portion of her dominions, and was so inordinately fond of everything Scotch, that even the English grew jealous, when year after year the Sovereign's chief desire seemed to be to prove that she possessed no English sympathies whatever, and that she positively declined to show the light of her countenance to any but Scotch subjects or German relatives, if she could help it.

The principal emoluments of the State fell to the share of alien Germans, and British taxpayers were ground to the dust, while scores of thousands of pounds of their money crossed the Channel for the support of Germans, some of whom were not too illustriously born, but all of whom found favour in the eyes of Victoria Regina.

A great deal of encouragement being thus given to the Germans and Scots, who were always willing to accept conditions to which the English found it impossible to bow, England became over-run with them, so much so, indeed, that the natives of the soil found it necessary to emigrate to other countries, in order to earn their livelihood, and England itself gradually became the principal abiding-place of a hybrid race, who were known as Teuto-Scots.

All this time Ireland languished in a state of neglect and discontent, which was eventually fanned into a fierce flame in consequence of the treatment bestowed by the English Government upon certain patriots whom they revered. There were several facsimile copies of allegorical documents which so evidently referred to events which occurred in my own time in England, and which were so prominently instanced as the predisposing causes of the Irish revolution, that I subsequently took the trouble of copying one of them, and give it in full as follows:—

Carolus Patriotus.
A Political Allegory.

And lo! there dwelt in this country a man whose name was Carolus. And this Carolus, who was surnamed Patriotus, looked with bitterness upon the wickedness of the oppressor, and said unto his friends and disciples, "Verily, I can no longer look upon the tribulations of my people, but will gird up my loins, and will set forth on a pilgrimage to the land of the oppressor."

And behold after many days he came to Londinensis, the chief city of the Albionites, and saw that which was not good in his sight. But he met many people who sate him at their board, and who looked upon him as the deliverer of his people. Unto them he said, "Verily, I will lift up my voice, so that it shall be heard of all the nations. And I will open the eyes of the people, so that they shall no longer look with favour upon the evil doings of their chief rulers. And I will say unto them, 'Cast your eyes upon Erinea, the country of my forefathers, and behold how my brethren gnash their teeth, and struggle in vain under the yoke of the spoiler and misruler.' And I will call upon them to give me their help in the deliverance of my people. And my nation shall bless those who lift up their voices for Erinea."

And behold all these things came to pass.

And the friends of Carolus, surnamed Patriotus, said unto him, "It is well that thou shouldest do this great thing. And, verily, we will aid thee. Our houses shall be thy houses, and our purses shall be thy purses, until the great things which thou prophesiest shall come to pass."

And Carolus, surnamed Patriotus, lifted up his voice against the oppressor, yea, even in the assembly of the rulers of the Albionites did he lift up his voice, and many disciples followed him.

But there was a great prince in Londinensis, the chief city of the Albionites, who waxed wroth at the preachings of Carolus, and who looked upon his teachings as evil. The name of this prince was Tempus Londinus, and he said unto his servants, "Yea, verily, this Carolus is a seditious man, and we must banish him from the great house of the people, else will he conquer us, and the power of the Albionites will be as naught in the eyes of the nations."

And there came unto the steward of Tempus, surnamed Londinus, a man named Dupus Journalius. This man longed for riches, and knew much that was pleasing to the steward of Tempus. Unto him he saith, "Lo, thy servant hath travelled far to satisfy thy desires, and to please my lord the prince. He has been to the chief city of the Erinians, and has spoken to a man who dwells there. This man has a sword, made by Carolus, and nothing but the poison which is worked into this sword can destroy Carolus, surnamed Patriotus. Carolus made this sword in order to destroy his enemies, but lo! he is now himself in their toils, and shall feel the hand of the smiter."

And the steward of the mighty Tempus said unto Dupus, he that was surnamed Journalius, "Fetch this man hither, that we may behold this weapon."

But Dupus answered and said, "Not so, my lord, for this thing is wonderful, and Judas Dublinus will not sell it but for a great price. Yea, verily, the price is great."

Then said the chief steward unto Dupus, "Go thy way, and return unto me tomorrow, when thou shalt see the mighty prince Tempus and his high priests, and they shall give thee an answer."

And when Dupus returned on the morrow, he prostrated himself before Tempus Londinus and his high priests, and they looked with favour upon him, and gave him great wealth, saying, "Go thou to Judas, surnamed Dublinus, and give him of thy wealth, and say unto him, 'Verily I have spoken of thee to the rulers of the Albionites, and thou and thy doings have found favour in their sight. Moreover, thou shalt not be punished for thy sins, but if thou wilt render unto me the poisoned sword wherewith to destroy Carolus, surnamed Patriotus, thou shalt dwell in the tents of the righteous.'"

And Dupus journeyed to the chief city of the Erinians, and told all those things unto Judas, surnamed Dublinus, who answered and said, "Yea, verily, my lord hath done well by his servant. Here is the sword which shall destroy Carolus, surnamed Patriotus."

Therefore Dupus was filled with joy, and hastened to carry the sword to the mighty prince of the Albionites. And the prince was well pleased with him, and many of the chief rulers of the people also rejoiced with him, saying unto each other, "Now we shall be delivered from the teachings of this vile impostor, and our country shall prosper, for the false prophet of Erinia is vanquished, and his disciples shall be scattered over all the earth."

But lo! and behold! a wonder came to pass. For when the high priests of Tempus Londinus hurled the poisoned sword, which Carolus was said to have wrought with his own hands, yea, when it was hurled at Carolus, he valiantly seized the sword, and fought his enemies therewith, so that those who thought to see him fall dead were amazed at his vigour.

But although Carolus did not die, he was sick for many days, and many people prophesied that his end was near, while his enemies said, "Rejoice, and be glad, for the foe is slain, and our enemies are crestfallen and hang their heads in shame!"

But there were others who said, "Nay, he shall not die, but shall live to plant the foot of scorn upon the neck of his enemy. We will give freely of our treasure, and we will carry him to the great apothecary, Carolus Magnus, and lo! he will heal his wounds, and lay bare the foul sores of the slanderers."

And all the Erinians cried aloud unto Carolus Magnus, saying, "Save our apostle, and let him not perish under the heel of his enemy."

Now Carolus, surnamed Magnus, was skilled in the art of healing, and it came to pass after many days that Carolus, surnamed Patriotus, recovered from his grievous sickness, and henceforth the great prince and his high priests looked with disfavour upon Dupus Journalius.

And Tempus Londinus was exceeding wroth, and sent for Judas, surnamed Dublinus. But the heart of Judas was filled with fear, so that he repented him of what he had done, and wandered afar off, sending unto Tempus and his high priests a message, saying, "Verily, I am a sinner, and have led a mighty prince into error. The sword which should have destroyed Carolus, surnamed Patriotus, was of a truth poisoned, but the poison lurks in the hilt, not in the point, of the weapon. If my lord falls sick thereof, let him not blame his servant Judas, who was tempted by the promise of great riches. And where Judas goes, let no man follow."

And the people clamoured for vengeance upon Judas and the hunters were set upon the track of the betrayer and he fell into their hands. But when they took their eyes from him, he sprang into the outermost darkness, and the inhabitants of the earth knew him no more.

And Tempus Londinus was in his turn grievously sick. But as for Carolus Patriotus, he grew mightier than ever, and there was rejoicing in Erinia when he triumphed over his enemies.

IV

B ut although this Carolus Patriotus was thus allegorically announced to be the victor, his country still suffered for a long time at the hands of its rulers. Disaffection and jealousy, increased in many places by the disinclination of the discontented ones to relieve themselves honourably of their burdens, caused certain practices to arise in Erinia or Ireland, which only aggravated the reigning misery.

A custom called "boycotting" prevailed, whereby all those who were suspected or proved to be unpatriotic were deprived of all communication with those who might possibly be induced to do business with them. People caught conveying food or other necessaries to boycotted persons were ruthlessly shot, and very often horrible cruelties were perpetrated upon harmless cattle, in order to show that their owners had fallen under the ban.

Morality became a thing unknown in the country. Farms and houses were rented from landholders, who had no other source of income, by people who meant to live upon the produce of the land, but who were resolved not to pay anything for the privilege. This was accounted quite an honourable thing to do, and the worst crime of which an Irish farmer could be accused of being guilty was "paying his rent."

Murder was an excusable necessity, but rent-paying was a crime punishable by death. Hence landlords found no encouragement to prove themselves deserving of confidence. Whole estates went to rack and ruin. The really earnest reformers found it impossible to fight longer against the prevailing misery, and emigrated in large numbers, so that the country at last fell into a state of complete anarchy.

There were many politicians whose sole exertions were directed towards securing to Ireland privileges which would put it on an equal footing with the sister isle, but other troubles fell upon Great Britain, and, as had often happened before, the affairs of Ireland were set aside in order that other grave difficulties might be grappled with.

Several British colonies and dependencies became alienated. The whole of the Australian dependencies threw off the yoke of England. The French became the ultimate possessors of Newfoundland, owing to the supineness of the Government to which it looked for protection. A treaty between the United States and France was the means of robbing England of Canada, and in order to prevent the loss of further slices of the Empire, Great Britain was obliged to maintain a large standing army and navy.

There were a great many republicans in the House of Commons, and these people always played upon one string. They urged that all the troubles and worries of the English had their origin in the huge sums of money which were paid to the Royal family, which ever grew more exacting and rapacious in its demands for money. So powerfully did the republicans appeal to the nation that many of the royalists began to consider the situation anxiously, and feared lest the reigning dynasty should be dethroned, and England be turned into a republic.

Others, however, considered that so much had been done to conciliate the Germans and Scots, who were both brave and of great skill in warfare, that an alliance with them could be safely counted upon in the event of a civil war breaking out.

Meanwhile France was also the scene of great political changes. The people had once more tired of the republic, and, with their usual extremeness, had once more rejoiced at the coronation of an Emperor. Bourbonists, Orleanists, and Bonapartists were alike powerless in the election of a supreme ruler, and their respective claims were all set on one side in favour of an obscure adventurer, who, emulating Napoleon, had used the army as the step-ladder for his ambition. The French nation, jealous of the fast-increasing power of its big German neighbour, gladly placed in supreme command a man who, among other things, promised to make the hated Teuton lick the dust.

Russian Autocracy was fast becoming a thing of the past, but Germany steadily grew in power, until it threatened to emulate the days of Charlemagne, and engulph all the countries between which it was sandwiched.

Such was the condition of some of the principal countries of Europe when the Irish, resolved no longer to "groan under the yoke of the oppressor," formed themselves into a secret society which embraced nearly all the nation; held many clandestine meetings, at which all manner of dark things were plotted; and finally invoked the aid of France in a grand fight which they were going to make for independence and freedom.

France readily agreed to the alliance, the proposal having apparently come at a most opportune time. The French always thirst for power; they are somewhat credulous as a nation; and are so vain as to be continually overestimating their own might and prowess. Add to this, that their Emperor was still new fledged, and still had to fulfil his promises of aggrandizement, and it will readily be believed that there was little difficulty in persuading France to become Ireland's ally in her crusade against England.

Not that France was honestly bent upon unselfishly befriending another country. It was thought that, once firmly fixed on Irish soil, with an army in occupation, it was simply a question of changing the absolute rulership of the Emerald Isle in favour of Gallia. Certain emoluments and prerogatives were to be given to the principal Irish leaders, as a sop to Cerberus, but the principal plums of conquest were to be reserved for Frenchmen, as soon as *"Albion la perfide"* was fairly vanquished.

Glorious visions of coming wealth and greatness filled the minds of the thousands who, led by the brand-new Emperor himself, swarmed into Ireland, and prepared, in conjunction with their red-hot allies, to smash England's greatness into infinitesimal fragments. Naturally the army was *fêted* and entertained, but it was unfortunate that so much of the product of the native distilleries should have been consumed in drinking confusion to their enemies, for Bacchus always was, and always will be, a treacherous friend, and he had something to answer for respecting the ruin, utter, black, and entire, which erelong overtook his votaries.

As England's statesmen had foreseen, they were able to count upon mighty aid from the Scots and Germans, and in their opinion the issue of the forthcoming struggle was a foregone conclusion. But Germany had to be very wary and circumspect, for Russia and Austria considered this a capital time to combine with France and bring about the disruption of the big German Empire. There was even a treaty signed, by virtue of which the three allied emperors were to share Germany very equitably, in event of conquest.

They counted upon Switzerland remaining neutral, but were slightly taken aback when Italy's army, which was now a very large one, was placed at the disposal of England and Germany, thus enabling the latter country to render powerful help to England, without imperilling its own safety very much.

The war did not last long. When Ireland struck the blow for liberty, both Irish and French fought well; the former goaded by desperation and a desire for revenge; the latter by cupidity and vain-gloriousness. But their valour was futile, and there came a day when their united forces were utterly vanquished, and scarcely an Irish or French soldier was left to show that there had once been a united army.

Fortunately for himself, the Emperor was slain in battle. Otherwise, with nothing but a list of ignominious defeats to show in what manner he had been able to keep his brilliant promises, he would have been disgraced by a nation that was once more enraged at having shown how huge was its capacity for being duped.

It soon transpired, however, that the residue of the French people had need to think of something else besides avenging failures. The enemies of France seized their opportunity; invaded it; conquered it; and divided it, undeterred by the pusillanimous threats of Russians and Austrians, who judged it wisest not to take to arms when the situation of France grew so desperate.

Thus did France cease to be an independent European power, and thus also were finally exterminated the Irish as a nation, for they were brave, and did not yield, so long as a man could fight.

In England there was great rejoicing, and so many honours were heaped upon Germans and Scots, that there was not an opening left for an Englishman to lift himself into prominence. The Government of the country gradually fell entirely into the hands of these aliens, and Englishmen formed so small a minority of the population that a proposal to change the name of the country from England to Teuto-Scotland was placed before Parliament, and carried by acclamation.

All record of England, so far as its constitutional policy was concerned, finished here, and I know not whether a ruler in the direct line of succession remained upon the throne, or whether a republic was the immediate outcome of all these changes or not. I learnt subsequently, however, from the lips of Hilda, that at the time of my visit to New Amazonia, the chief officer of state in Teuto-Scotland was a "People's Agent," who only remained two years in office, and was then replaced by such successor, either male or female, as might be elected by universal suffrage.

V

Since the Irish people had been completely conquered, it behoved England to take such measures as would conduce to the future prosperity of the island, and at the same time guard against disaffection and rebellion. There was much consulting and advising. The Irish question was as prominent as ever. All manner of plans were proposed, but were all in turn rejected as unfeasible.

After several sessions had been wasted in fruitless debates and in noisy discussions, whereof the only result arrived at was a certain amount of forensic display on the part of ambitious members, a proposition was mooted which at first amazed all who heard it. Then it was ridiculed unmercifully. Next it was discussed seriously. Finally it was adopted, amid universal enthusiasm.

For centuries the combined effects of war, seafaring, and emigration had been to reduce the male population of England to such an extent as to cause the female portion of the population to preponderate enormously. So much so, in fact, that not a trade or profession which had hitherto been regarded by men as sacred to themselves was uninvaded by feminine competitors, who, considerably to the dismay of adult masculinity, were steadily proving themselves capable of doing well all that they undertook to do.

For every man in the community to support three women was an impossibility, even if he had desired to do so, which he certainly did not. Women who did not marry were expected to keep themselves. But by way of showing how strictly and impartially just the male biped can be, there prevailed a peculiar system of payment, which bore its natural result of discontent and protest.

For instance, in Messrs. Workemphast's establishment several women were engaged as assistants. They performed their work more neatly and deftly than their masculine rivals, but were paid only half as much for their services, simply because they were women. The result in all such cases was that other expensive men were ousted to make room for some more underpaid women, the consequence being that none but the employers were satisfied.

The men had an idea that although it was only right that woman should not be a burden on man, she had no business to invade his particular province of labour. The women, on the other hand, considered themselves entitled to equal pay with the men, provided their work was equal.

On other grounds, too, they had ample cause for complaint. Women householders were compelled to pay quite as heavy rates and taxes as men, but were debarred from every privilege to which equal payment of tribute morally entitled them. Although made to provide the necessary funds for governing the country, they were not merely debarred from holding office, but were even prohibited from having a voice in the election of such members of the favoured sex as aspired to be the rulers of the land.

A woman might pay a large share of her income towards the expenses of the Government. She might employ a dozen servants, such as gardeners, grooms, coachmen, gamekeepers, etc., but although each of the men dependent upon her for a livelihood, no matter how stupid, ignorant, or loutish they might be, was accorded the privilege of voting, their clever, accomplished mistress was considered to belong to an inferior order of beings, to whom it would be unwise to accord privileges, seeing that they were not supposed to have sufficient sense to use these privileges wisely.

Again. Adultery alone on the part of a wife was quite sufficient ground for a divorce in favour of the husband, but a wife must have a husband who, in addition to being persistently and openly unfaithful, cruelly ill-treated her, and took a cowardly advantage of the superiority of strength he had attained through having systematically deprived woman of every health-giving recreation, before the law, made by men for the benefit of men, would afford her relief from her daily tortures.

It is on record that a judge, when a woman was being tried for the presumed murder of her husband, dwelt with such horror upon the most dreadful fact that she had been unfaithful to her husband, and proved so conclusively that a woman who could be unfaithful was capable of every crime under the sun, that the jury, remembering that their interests as husbands must be protected, sentenced the woman to be hanged, although medical witnesses showed that she could not be a murderess, seeing that the cause of her husband's death was a drug of which he was proved to have been a systematic partaker.

From this it will be argued that purity of living held high rank with the English. But this was by no means the case, for in the same decade the rebellion and protests of women were naturally aroused by the foulest and most disgusting legislation that ever disgraced the land. This was the State regulation of vice, whereby the most respectable women were liable to be subjected to brutal indignities, in order that no precaution might be neglected which would ensure for men complete immunity from the consequences of systematic libertinism and immorality.

This may sound paradoxical, but it is not the less sickening in its shameful reality, and serves to show the hollowness and insincerity of masculine legislators.

It is small wonder that these and other crying evils brought forth the fruits they did. Systematic injustice roused the antipathy of women who, besides having sense enough to argue their own case, had sufficient moral courage to brave the animadversion which was levelled at them by the arrogant idiots of the one sex, and the unreasoning imbeciles of the other.

Hence the expressions which we come across at times, which to modern New Amazonians unacquainted with history are unintelligible, but which had their own bitter meaning at the time they were in use. "Bluestocking" was a term of opprobrium levelled at women who strove to improve their moral and intellectual status by means of study. A "Woman's Rights' Advocate" was described as an individual who was the fit butt for the laughter and derision of the rest of the community.

To be strong-minded was a wonderful claim to respect in a man. Men were fond of speaking of women as the "weak-minded," and, therefore, inferior sex, and yet the moment a woman proved herself to be not *weak*-minded but *strong*-minded, she was regarded as an anomaly, and sneered at as a being who had unsexed herself. To be "only a woman" was equivalent in the minds of many male egotists to being only "something better than his dog, and something dearer than his horse," and yet, no sooner did she prove herself gifted with abilities hitherto cherished as exclusively masculine, and, therefore, infinitely superior to womanly attributes, than she was said to have become "masculine," and regarded as an object of horror. To be a woman was to be one unit of a despised race, and yet to "unsex" herself was one of the most opprobrious faults of which a woman could be guilty!

Could anything be more idiotic or paradoxical? And is it to be wondered at that it became necessary for men to *prove* their vaunted superiority? And that they were gradually impelled, from sheer fear of the future, to grant the demands of the sex which was rapidly learning to estimate itself at its true value?

No struggle recorded in history can compare with the fight against oppression which was now carried on by the brave and noble ancestresses of whom we have such good reason to be proud. Many and disheartening were the defeats they endured, but gloriously triumphant was their final victory, of which our existence as an independent nation was the outcome.

Universal Suffrage! Wonderful was the jubilation when it became an accomplished fact. And wonderful were its effects upon the nation. All the anomalies above described were wiped away, and women showed themselves so much more just, and so much more capable of governing than men, that they invariably enacted none but strictly fair and impartial regulations.

Thus Boards of Guardians consisted of an equal number of women and men. The latter superintended many details as formerly, but were relieved from the sole responsibility of seeing after the babies' feeding bottles, and the mothers' needs, and the old women's baths, which they had until now considered their own especial province.

Formerly none but male inspectors were allowed to perambulate the schools, at the expense of the country, and adjudicate as to the quality of make, and perfection of cut, of the underclothing for women which the girls were instructed to prepare for examination. Strange to say, it was not without considerable opposition that women were admitted to be fit to usurp this cherished masculine prerogative.

From time immemorial the fact that all doctors were men had proved a serious calamity, for thousands of women let their infirmities grow upon them until it was too late to save their lives, simply because they were reluctant to confide the details of their ailments to members of the other sex, who in most cases were complete strangers to them. And yet the universities were for ages shut in the face of women who were anxious to remedy these evils, and many and hard were the rebuffs and insults which were endured by the first women who succeeded in removing all barriers and in passing the examinations which qualified them as M.D.'s.

Houses were erected on principles which men regarded as perfect, but which women invariably found to be wofully deficient in matters appertaining to hygiene and comfort. Since women became architects these evils were also remedied, and as their augmented influence now penetrated everywhere, a great change of necessity came over the whole nation, and paved the way for one of the greatest political events the world has ever seen.

This was the resolve to colonise Ireland with the women who outnumbered the men so enormously in Teuto-Scotland.

It was duly remembered that the country had hitherto never managed to support itself, and that its periodical famines had been a source of enormous expense to Teuto-Scotland, which even now was voting large sums for the support of the widows and children of the men who had fallen in the late disastrous rebellion.

Many debates were, therefore, held respecting the annual amount which should henceforth be devoted to the maintenance of Teuto-Scottish authority in Ireland. But careful thought on the part of the greatest leaders of the colonisation movement resulted in the island being altogether given up to the sole rule and governance of the chief colonists. "Home Rule" was the watchword, and it was finally agreed that a treaty of alliance should be signed, whereby Ireland, or New Amazonia as it was henceforth called, should maintain friendly relations with the mother-country, but should be a perfectly self-governing and independent State, exempt from any allegiance but that of friendliness, and a mutual desire to prevent the encroachments of foreigners.

In return for so immense a concession, it was stipulated that New Amazonia should now be self-supporting, and very few but enthusiasts, remembering the past history of the island, believed in anything but a total collapse of the new government.

Fortunately for our land, there were vast numbers of enthusiastic believers in the available resources of New Amazonia, and in the capacity of its chosen leaders, so that the fifty millions of pounds, with which it was necessary to be equipped, in order to start the new enterprise on a sound basis, was raised in a remarkably short time.

Three and a half percent consols were issued, and were eagerly bought up by the enormous numbers of women who desired to become colonists in the new republic, and to partake of the advantages and opportunities, which would then be theirs. Great financiers were also found willing to become partners in this novel syndicate, and as the consols were bought up in every European country, every European country was directly interested in the prosperity of New Amazonia, and the spirit and courage of its leaders was the prominent topic of conversation in the whole of the civilised world.

VI

It was intended that the government should consist of a Leader, two Prime Advisers, twelve Privy Counsellors, and two hundred-and-fifty Tribunes, all elected by the people. As a preliminary measure, however, only fifty Inaugurators were chosen by the Teuto-Scottish Parliament, and upon these devolves the selection of the swarms of women who clamoured to become members of the new republic. The Inaugurators were divided into five committees, consisting of ten members each. These were named respectively the Financial, the Medical, the Social, the Political, and the Religious.

The Financial Committee was the first which the candidate had to face. No woman was accepted for membership who could not invest a certain sum of money in New Amazonian consols. This rule served a twofold purpose. It prevented the intrusion of women whose poverty would make them a burden to the rest of the community, which above all things required a fair start. And, by making every member a partner in the monetary venture, it ensured the personal interest of every inhabitant of the country in its permanent prosperity.

The Medical Committee was next entrusted with a careful examination of all those who had been able to satisfy Committee number one. Every woman who bore the slightest trace of disease or malformation about her was rigorously rejected, and those who passed the second stage satisfactorily were handed over to the tender mercies of the Social Committee, whose mission it was to enquire into the antecedents of the candidates, and weed out such as were likely to prove discreditable to the rest.

Few of the women, having reached this stage of the examinations, found any difficulty in agreeing to the conditions of committees four and five. They were simply required to take an oath of allegiance to the new government, and to swear to obey any laws or rules which might be made by the Constitution. They also vowed to merge all religious differences, and to conform to whatever religious doctrines might be ultimately agreed upon as a safe basis for the establishment of a national church.

When all these preliminaries were duly gone through, the candidate paid her money, received satisfactory security for it, signed certain documents, and was henceforth a duly enrolled citizen of New

Amazonia, pledged to respect all its laws, and entitled to participate in all its benefits.

When the inaugural committees, satisfied that the enterprise could now be floated without further delay, decided to remove the scene of their operations to Dublin, as the capital city of the new republic had hitherto been called, there was great excitement in London.

A banquet was given in honour of the pioneers of the movement, and the Teuto-Scottish Government entered so cordially into the spirit of the great enterprise, as to ensure free travelling expenses to their future home to all accepted New Amazonians who were willing to avail themselves of the privilege.

In many cases this was a great boon, for although no men were accepted as colonists, the future was provided for by the admission of all the healthy children of enrolled citizens. As only a small proportion of the adventurers were women who had been married, the number of children was small enough to be comfortably provided for.

Proclamations had been issued announcing many benefits which were to fall to the lot of the very small remnant of the Irish nation, and it was anticipated that when they found themselves to be enjoying equal privileges with the new comers they would lose the resentful demeanour they had hitherto maintained, and be amenable to the dictates of kindness and reason.

It was many years, however, before the last flickerings of their discontent were extinguished, and before they could be induced to take kindly to the mode of living universally enforced throughout the country. This end being finally attained, the mingled races became amalgamated, and were henceforth alike devoted to their country and its constitutional laws.

It was well for New Amazonia in the end that a good many Irish women had survived, for the arts of linen-making and lace-making, which they perpetuated and improved, are among the most valuable sources of revenue of the country.

Shortly after the Inaugurators were established in Dublin Castle a general election was called, and all the members of the Constitution were duly elected. These elections were to be triennial, none of the officials to be eligible for two successive Parliaments. The country was divided into two hundred and fifty districts, each of which elected its own Tribune, and paid for the maintenance of that Tribune during her term of office.

The salaries of the Leader, Prime Advisers, and Privy Councillors were fixed upon a progressive basis, and were payable by the State. The National Revenue was a question which required much anxious thought, but a solution of the problem was eventually arrived at, which was in course of time supplemented by the present existing arrangements.

The State was to be the only importer, no private competition being permitted. Hence the question of excise became a thing of the past.

The appointment of a great many officials to regulate the export and import trade was necessitated, and this at once gave employment to hundreds of receiving and exporting agents, who in their turn required the services of clerks.

All the goods which arrived in the country were paid for by the State, and transferred at a percentage of profit to wholesale merchants with capital enough to pay for large business transactions of this nature. Careful tariffs were drawn up, and the maximum of profit chargeable by the State upon all goods labeled as "Necessaries" was five percent "Luxuries," however, all yielded twenty percent profit to the State.

From the hands of the wholesale merchant all goods were transferred to retail dealers, and by them placed within the reach of the people at large. In order to prevent the largest capitalists from absorbing the whole of the national trade, different branches were not permitted to be adopted by one merchant or retail dealer.

Thus no draper was allowed to sell groceries, furniture, ironmongery, stationery, or anything else which did not legitimately appertain to the drapery business, and other traders were restricted by similar regulations. By adopting this method the State prevented one or two firms from making huge fortunes at the expense of fifty less opulent traders, as was the case in Teuto-Scotland, where the system of compound establishments, syndicates, and corners prevailed to a disastrous extent.

At first the export traffic was not large, but was regulated in a similar manner to the import trade. The State was the ultimate receiver, and final vendor of all goods exported, a percentage of profit being exacted on all goods sent away.

As the trade of the country, stimulated by the energy and determination of its new inhabitants, steadily increased, the revenues derived by the State were enormous, and no other method of taxation was deemed necessary. We thus have, for the first time, the spectacle of a highly civilised country in which the tax-collector is non-existent.

As every sort of employment which presented itself had to be done by women, the question of a convenient working attire, which should at the same time be suitable, healthy, warm, and becoming, was soon brought up for discussion.

After much debate and strenuous opposition on the part of some advocates of changeable fashions, it was decided to adopt a national distinctive dress, the wearing of which should be compulsory. Latter day New Amazonians find it difficult to believe that the barbarous mode of dressing which had prevailed among the English, and later among the Teuto-Scots, was reluctantly abandoned by thousands of women, and that the New Amazonian National dress should have been strenuously objected to at first.

There is in the museum, at Garrettville, an instrument of torture on exhibition called a corset. Its extreme width is eighteen inches, and it is an almost incredible fact that this instrument once spanned the waist of a woman, who was only following one of the maddest and silliest fashions ever instituted, when she deliberately forced her ribs out of their proper places, and prepared an early grave for herself, in order that she might meet with the favour of some idiot of the other sex, who preferred fashion and doctor's bills to health and happiness.

The children who came with their mothers to New Amazonia were housed in existing large buildings, until suitable erections for their reception could be designed and built. Their supervision and education was for a time entrusted to the mothers, subject to the directions of a trained staff of teachers.

Physical education was all that was aimed at until the child's tenth birthday had been passed. The most careful attention was paid to diet, the necessary proportions of heat, flesh, and starch-formers being supplied to them, all cooked in such palatably scientific methods as conduced to build up a perfect system.

Swimming, running, dancing, drill, gymnastics, and every physical health-giving game in vogue constituted the curriculum of youngsters under ten. In the old country, thousands of little ones were pining from bodily lassitude and decay engendered by the brain work necessitated by a senseless system of cramming and examining. In New Amazonia the children entering school at the age of ten were splendidly robust; had a healthy, strong mind in a healthy, strong body, and were capable, without fatigue, of learning more in two years than their Teuto-Scottish contemporaries learned in all the seven years they had been compelled to attend school.

For six years the school course had to be pursued, then a choice of trade or profession adapted to the abilities of the student was made. The next four years were devoted to the learning of this trade, and the earnings of the next five years were appropriated by the State, which thus remunerated itself for the heavy expense of maintaining and educating each of its subjects under twenty years of age.

At the age of twenty-five each subject was at liberty to appropriate her earnings as she liked, but was also expected to provide her own board and residence henceforth.

As no men were admitted to any of the chief offices, some of them emigrated, but others were glad to remain, and adopted various trades which rendered them acceptable and useful members of the community. In course of time, a desire was manifested on the part of several couples to cast in their lot together, and it became necessary to pay some attention to the marriage laws, which, as they had existed in Teuto-Scotland, were totally rejected by New Amazonians as altogether obsolete, and stupidly conducive to crime and immorality. The marriage contract, under the new code of laws, became a purely civil one, dissolvable almost without cost, upon one or other of the parties to it proving incompatibility or unfaithfulness on the part of the other.

A document, received by each of the divorcees, legally entitled them to marry again, provided they fulfilled every other necessary condition. A medical certificate of soundness had to be procured before anyone was allowed to marry, as, above all, the State was determined to secure none but healthy subjects.

Sometimes very painful scenes were witnessed, for each new-born child was subjected to examination, and no crippled or malformed infants were permitted to live.

As all children were considered the property of the State, neither wife nor husband was responsible for their maintenance and education, and when a divorce was in prospect it was not necessary to take the offspring of the temporary union into consideration at all, though no divorces were permitted until after the birth of any expected result of such union. Nursing mothers were always welcomed with their children, and were maintained by the State, so long as the latter required their attendance.

There was, however, a determination on the part of the Government to guard against the evils of over-population in the future, and Malthusian doctrines were stringently enforced. Any woman or man

ELIZABETH BURGOYNE CORBETT

becoming the parent of more than four children was punished for such recklessness by being treated as a criminal, and deprived of many very valuable civil rights.

It had often been the objection of legislators in the old country that Woman's Suffrage would, in some never satisfactorily explained manner, cause an access of immorality in the land, seeing that immoral women would have as much right to vote as their more virtuous sisters. The stupidity and selfishness of such an argument is easily deducible from the fact that a large number of the male members themselves were men who led anything but moral lives.

Health of body, the highest technical and intellectual knowledge, and purity of morals has ever been the goal aimed at in New Amazonia, and it can today boast of being the most perfect, the most prosperous, and the most moral community in existence.

VII

There existed many places of worship in the country, which were at first used indiscriminately by Catholics, Protestants, Jews, Wesleyans, Presbyterians, Quakers, and a host of other sects whose varied religious beliefs were so perplexing and confusing, and provocative of so many quarrels and discussions, that sectarianism was soon recognized as the rock upon which the nation was likely to founder, unless prompt legislation was brought to bear upon the situation.

Some believed in a Trinity of Gods, some in a Unity. Others looked forward to the coming of a Redeemer, others worshipped Jesus Christ, as the Redeemer of souls. Some denied a God altogether, and asserted that all the higher forms of life were the outcome of evolution. Others, again, worshipped a goddess called Humanity, and all were more or less in fear of a mythical Being to whom all the untold millions born into the world were supposed to be turned over for everlasting punishment in the event of their not having been fortunate enough to meet with all the requirements of creeds formulated by men.

Thus, one portion of the community had been taught that tiny babes, dying before they had been sprinkled with water by a priest, and had a certain formula of words uttered over them, would be consigned to everlasting perdition, and debarred from all the joys of a future life. Others would have been brought up to believe that all the untold millions of people who had, by force of circumstances, over which they had not the slightest control, never had Christianity preached to them, would also be delivered into the hands of Satan!

Could anything be more blasphemously opposed to the character of a merciful Creative Being, than to suppose it capable of producing myriads of human beings, simply that they might be consigned to never-ending torture such as only fiends could sanction?

Bigotry, Sectarianism, and Dogmatic Obstinacy had taken the place of a true and simple worship of the Creator. So rank did the strife become that certain sects actually maintained it to be wicked to enter a place of worship patronised by a rival sect. So truly religious were the majority of Christians that they only used the various churches as a means of advancing their temporal power, and statistics from all the world will prove that more lives have been lost, and more crimes committed, in the name of Religion, than from any other cause. Strange that what should be regarded as the greatest bond of unity upon earth should be so abused as to become one of its greatest powers for evil! Yet so it was when our forerunners peopled this land, and they were compelled to adopt stringent methods of grappling with the most serious evil in their midst.

The earth was too beautiful, and life itself was too great a mystery for the doctrine of a bounteous Creator to be entirely abandoned, so worship was offered, and temples dedicated, to the service of "The Giver of Life," who was always pictured as loving and beneficent, and to whom no fearful qualities were attributed such as for ages made professing Christians live a life of fear lest they should really not be saved, and caused those who were taught to regard themselves as transgressors to die a death of horror and despair.

The doctrines preached henceforth were "Gratitude" to the "Giver of Life," and the "Duty" to others of leading a pure and moral existence. A simple creed this, but one which all were ultimately able to adopt, and the worship of Morality never had any other effect upon the worship of "Life-Giver" than to render it all the more sincere and heartfelt.

All fear of a future state is banished from the minds of New Amazonians, who refuse to believe in a Prince of Darkness, and discard the doctrine of everlasting punishment entirely. A continuance of life hereafter is firmly believed in, the goal of bliss being supposed to be the ultimate perfection which will make the soul so glorious in knowledge and purity as to bring it near to "Life-Giver" herself, and enable it to revel in the supreme happiness afforded to all who have left ignorance and imperfection behind.

A priesthood was established after a time in New Amazonia, but was bereft of the especial privileges hitherto deemed inseparable from that holy office, but which were now regarded as the principal causes of the corruption, perversion of truth, and immorality which prevailed in the churches of Teuto-Scotland and other countries. No salary was attached to the office whatever, and thus religion was deprived of its chief means of abuse, for formerly disreputable persons who could command influence were not debarred from choosing the sacred office of priest, and from drawing the large profits which in many cases were derivable from their appointment.

In Teuto-Scotland the Church was simply regarded as an easy and lucrative profession. In New Amazonia it is an honour only bestowed upon capable people, who already possess a sufficient income to enable them to dispense with a further addition to it.

The doctrines they have to expound are simple, and their principal duty consists in providing Professors, each of high repute in their various professions, to lecture at different periods of that day, which is still, in accordance with ancient usage, set apart as the day of general cessation from ordinary toil.

Since it is not given one soul to be perfect in everything, and since the attempted study of everything would result in perfection in nothing, each individual hopes to become more speedily sure of final perfection by using all available means of improvement in what is at present the chief business of life, and by attending the lectures provided by the Guardian for the purpose of elucidating the most intricate technicalities of each trade and profession in existence.

The Lecturers are chosen by the State, and are all paid a uniform salary. As many places would be too small to repay for the domiciling of a complete staff of Lecturers in their midst, a system of travelling prevails, whereby the Lecturers travel from one place to another, so that each member of the community may have opportunities of attaining individual perfection by receiving public instruction in her or his special vocation.

All railways, water companies, and similar great undertakings are in the hands of the State, which receives all surplus profits, and pays its employés more liberally than private companies ever did in former days. A fixed percentage is always taken by the State. Should the proceeds be more than the State percentage, the surplus becomes the perquisite of the working staff, who thus receive a graduated addition to their income. Should bad work or bad management reduce the profits, the State still takes its fixed percentage, and it is thus made the individual interest of all persons employed by the State to do their best to promote the success of whatever department of State labour is entrusted to them.

The Teuto-Scots were guilty of many practices which are rigorously prohibited in New Amazonia. One of these was the use of the dried leaves of a plant called tobacco; by some it was put in the mouth, and the juice masticated out of it. By the majority of users it was slowly burnt, and the resulting smoke allowed to pass into the mouth, to be emitted immediately after in clouds of an unpleasant, choking nature. The practice is in many old works described as dirty and offensive; yet it is an undoubted fact that the discontinuance of the use of tobacco was so rebelled against, and so distasteful to many New Amazonian women, that frequent expulsions from the country took place before the custom was stamped out.

In all times there have been many vices attributed to the habit of imbibing fluids, which were so remarkable in their effects, that the users of them were deprived of both sense and motion, besides suffering bodily illness. It is the boast of New Amazonia that an intoxicant cannot be procured in the island, and that all existing establishments for the manufacture of these dangerous compounds were devoted to more noble uses.

The majority of Teuto-Scots were carnivorous, like dogs, cats, and birds of prey. Flesh eating is a habit which induces coarseness of mind and body, and robs both of the true beauty, and vigour furnished by a vegetable diet. That Life-Giver never intended the human animal to be carnivorous is proved by the anatomy of the human frame.

It is, however, probable that New Amazonia became a vegetarian nation in consequence of the repugnance or inability of the first women who came over from Teuto-Scotland to kill the animals from whose carcases the beef, pork, and mutton they had hitherto consumed was obtained. They probably found it a great deprivation to subsist without a large proportion of animal food at first, and it was for a time extensively imported. Vegetarian and Humanitarian doctrines were extensively preached, and in course of time, as the art of cookery was more carefully cultivated, the trade in meat carcases ceased entirely, to the ultimate permanent advantage of the nation, than which no finer race exists in the world at this moment.

It is on record that the ancients paid great attention to the diet and housing of the animals intended either for slaughter, for beasts of burden, or for the chase, and that they knew exactly what food would produce the most coveted results. Thus they would subject their animals to one kind of treatment calculated to produce fat, while a change of diet would be productive of lean flesh. Any other results aimed at would be treated with corresponding acumen.

They even were able to produce a cruel disease in geese, whereby their livers were inordinately enlarged. These diseased livers were used in the construction of certain pies called *pâtés-de-fois-gras*, which were consumed in large quantities by those who could afford the high prices charged for them.

And yet, incredible as it may seem, these people had scarcely the most elementary knowledge of the necessary means of preserving the lives of their children, and rearing them in a methodical or scientific manner. No restraints were placed upon the people relative to the number of their offspring, for thousands of children died daily through the ignorance and incapacity of those who were entrusted with the rearing of them, thus partially counteracting one evil by the infliction of another, incalculable suffering being the invariable accompaniment of such mal-administration of mundane affairs.

If the offspring of the Teuto-Scots attained maturity, they were the subjects of such miseries as make New Amazonians often wonder how they supported life's burden. Their social pleasures were perpetually ruined by their inability to understand the signs of the weather until a tempest was upon them. Such a thing as altering the direction of a steady wind, and thereby producing either wet or fine weather, by means of a huge artificially created vacuum, had never been thought of. Neither had they attained the scientific knowledge which enables us to prevent disastrous thunderstorms by utilising all superfluous electricity, that would otherwise accumulate and work mischief.

So much was the life of the ancients dominated by the perpetual changes of weather in the British Islands, that it is said that no conversation ever took place in their day without some allusion to the weather being made in it.

Their lives were rendered unbearable by constant troubles which innumerable diseases wrought on their frames, and by the ever-recurring removal of some dear friend by death.

The advance of age was not looked for with delight and eagerness, as with us, for it brought with it an appalling train of evils. The body waxed feeble and bent. The eyes grew dim and often sightless. The senses of taste, smell, and hearing became impaired. The voice cracked, and made the speech harsh and shaky. The teeth fell out, after gradually and painfully decaying in the mouth. The gait became unsteady. The mind grew feeble, and the whole body was transformed into a pitiable spectacle of ruin and misery, soon to fall into the grave, unless one of the fell diseases to which these our ancestors were subjected swept them out of life long ere this.

Science was then in its infancy, and transfusion of blood was scouted as useless and impracticable, or many of the troubles of those days might have been avoided.

All these things were bad enough to endure, but when we remember that the greater part of the human race was led to expect nothing better after bodily death than a continuance of the spiritual ego in a state of horrible and never-ending torture, then indeed we may be thankful that we are free from so many of the ills to which it was then popularly believed all human flesh was heir.

VIII

I closed the book which I had been perusing, with a sense of the liveliest amazement. Was it possible, I thought, that this wonderful people had really conquered disease, decay, death, and the elements?

The suggestion seemed so wild, and my surroundings altogether were so strange, that I pinched myself to make sure that I had not really left my earthly casing behind me, and emerged, Chrysalis-like, into another world, whereof the grovelling nature of my former existence had failed to give me any conception.

But no, I was as sensitive to pain as ever I had been; and, to make the situation once more one of active reality, Hilda presently made her re-appearance. It was well for me that she seemed to have taken a strong fancy to me, otherwise I should never have been able to feel so much at ease in her presence as I did.

True, she was not more than nineteen years of age, so she told me, and was still pursuing the studies which were to qualify her to become a full-blown Lecturer on Chemical Science, but her physique was so splendid, and her mental qualities of such surprising vigour for one so young as she, that it was impossible for me to regard myself other than as a very inferior being in her presence.

She was very pleased to find that I had been able to read the books she had placed at my disposal; but her powers of belief were severely taxed when I insisted that the retrospect, referring to the peculiar habits and customs of the Ancients, was a faithful picture of things as they still existed in my own country.

"To tell you the truth," she said at last, "I think that you have been asleep for about six hundred years. You must have been taking Schlafstrank, though I had no idea it had been so long in existence."

"And, pray, what is Schlafstrank, and what are its uses?" I asked, whereupon I was told that Schlafstrank was an essence, discovered in the year 2239, by Ada of Garretville, while Senior Lecturer in Chemistry for that year. The uses to which this essence was devoted was to put people to sleep for a longer or a shorter period of time, according to the quantity inhaled or swallowed. While under the influence of Schlafstrank any amount of pain could be borne without causing the subject of it any real inconvenience, since no sense of pain or bodily suffering was conveyed to the sleeping mind.

Thus if, in unusual exception to the rule of perfect health which prevailed here, some dangerous or painful disease overtook any of the children of the State, be they old or young, they were subject to the influence of Schlafstrank, and then dosed or operated upon until the disease was conquered. In this way did New Amazonians avoid suffering, and it struck me as marvellous to picture them as the subjects of an accident resulting in a few broken limbs, and being unconscious of any inconvenience arising therefrom during the processes of setting and recovery. I was told that Schlafstrank produced no deleterious effect upon the body, although repeated doses were given, if the patient's mind threatened to awake before complete recovery of the body had set in.

One thing mystified me exceedingly. I was told that Schlafstrank was not invented until the year 2239, and naturally asked what year this was supposed to be. No doubt there was ample room for amusement on both sides when I positively averred that the year 1889 was not yet at an end, and Hilda insisted just as positively that this was the year 2472.

Not a little to my surprise, an attendant knocked at the door, and presented me with a parcel, with the words "From the Mother."

"The Mother?", I queried, and Hilda, pitying my ignorance, informed me that the State was the Mother of her people, and that no doubt the parcel contained a suitable outfit for me. On opening the parcel, I found the latter surmise to be correct, and I was eased of the last remnant of embarrassment I might have entertained at the idea of encroaching upon the hospitality of others, by being informed that it was considered a personal honour for any individual member of the State to be permitted to dispense the Mother's hospitality to all comers.

No stranger was permitted to seek private hospitality, but was provided, at the behest and expense of the Mother, with everything necessary for comfort while in New Amazonia.

I suggested that if this were generally known, the country was in danger of being over-run by loafers and adventurers of all nations.

This argument was met by the information that no strangers were permitted to land except such as showed good reason for their advent. If, by any chance, a person obtained access to the country who was inclined to abuse its hospitality, she or he was subjected to a course of labour which more than sufficed to pay expenses, and was then promptly expelled, one of the numerous fleet of trading steamers which New Amazonia now possessed being used as a means of transport to the culprit's own country.

ELIZABETH BURGOYNE CORBETT

Hilda's duties were not quite completed, but she told me that if I would induct myself in my new garments during her absence, she would return to me as soon as possible, and that she was deputed to inform me that Principal Grey and Professor Wise were prepared to escort me on a tour round the city, if I cared to go.

Es geht ohne sagen that I jumped at the offer, metaphorically speaking, and that I exerted myself to the utmost to transform my outward semblance by wasting no time ere I changed my own attire for the National costume a bountiful State had placed at my disposal. I availed myself of a marble bath which Hilda had shown me, and even half resolved to sacrifice my hair, in my desire to make myself as less like an oddity as possible.

The clothes proved a good fit, if the term could be applied to garments whose chief beauty consisted in the absolute freedom from constraint which they exercised over the body. I noticed one omission, which I was inclined to regret. No graceful sash formed part of my outfit, and I learnt afterwards that none but natives of the soil, or formally adopted immigrants, were permitted to adorn themselves with this distinctive National badge.

I was very much relieved when, on the return of Hilda, she pronounced me to be so passable as to be sure to escape the annoyance of being conspicuously Ancient looking, my diminutive stature being now the only specially noticeable feature about me, provided my hair could be hidden. Upon trial, my new velvet cap proved too inadequate a means of securing the desired end, and, with something akin to a pang, I must confess, I empowered Hilda to deprive me of what I had hitherto been taught to regard as woman's glory.

No sooner, however, was I bereft of all superabundant tresses, than I decided that the men who have from time to time so zealously exhorted women to wear their hair long, have done it from an innate conviction that the practice was debilitating and inconvenient, and therefore likely to prove an invaluable aid in the final subjugation of woman. Unlike Samson of old, I rejoiced in my newly acquired lack of hirsute adornment, and went on my way rejoicing.

I also found locomotion so much easier in my new attire, that the marble stairs had no terrors for me, and the interest I felt in all I saw proved a powerful incentive to exertion. I was not sorry to find that we were to be fortified with another meal before starting on our exploring expedition. As at the previous meal, there was no animal food, but the fare was scientifically perfect, and calculated to appeal powerfully to the senses by its appetising odour and appearance. Three meals per diem proved to be the rule here, and I observed that, compared to their physique, the appetites of the New Amazonians seemed to be very moderate. This was no doubt due to the fact that every item of food consumed was of such a nature that it at once supplied all the wants of the body, and that all indigestible or innutritive foods had long ago been banished from New Amazonian regimen as injurious on account of the useless waste of bodily force entailed in digesting or assimilating them.

I was, however, glad to find that tea was not condemned as entirely useless, and I thoroughly enjoyed this third and last meal of the day, after which I was taken out to explore posthumous Dublin, now called Andersonia. Once, when paying a flying visit to St. Petersburg, I was much struck by the large scale upon which all the principal streets and buildings were planned, and when I arrived in London, not very long after this, I felt positively relieved at the sight of the comparatively narrow and dingy London streets and buildings, and the sense of glare and unreality which made itself palpable in St. Petersburg promptly vanished in the atmosphere of London smoke.

Yellow-ochred palaces, lime-washed theatres, golden domes, and gaudy blue and white and gilt churches appealed less to my fancy than did the solid stone beauties of London architecture, grimy though they might be.

In looking upon Andersonia I was forcibly reminded of both the cities just mentioned. There were the same large, open squares, revealing broad, avenue-lined streets planned with mathematical exactitude, and the same huge buildings that I had noticed in St. Petersburg. But there was also the same solidity, freedom from glare, and honesty of composition, which roused my admiration when looking upon some of London's magnificent stone buildings. Here, however, were examples of architecture such as I had never before seen the like of for magnificence, and it was no detriment to their beauty that they were unsullied by smoke or dirt.

This seemed a very large city, and must have contained a numerous population, yet not one smoking chimney did I see. The weather was delightfully mild, but of course heat was necessary for cooking. In my ideas, a fire was just as necessarily associated with smoke, and I expressed my surprise at its evident absence. Considerably to my astonishment, I had some difficulty in making myself understood, but, in the end, mutual enlightenment was the result of our confabulations.

Electricity was made so thoroughly subservient to human will that it supplied light, heat, and powers of volition, besides being made to perform nearly every conceivable domestic use. So well were the elements analysed and understood here that thunderstorms were unknown, and the force which yearly used to slay numbers of people was now attracted, cooped, and subjugated to human necessities.

The skies were unclouded, the air delightfully bracing, the atmosphere so clear and pure that I wondered if some strange change had not occurred to my eyesight, since I could see miles and miles of fair country, lovely villages, and populous towns, whichever way I looked.

Smoke was an imponderable quantity here, by virtue of the smoke-consuming apparati fixed in every dwelling, which permitted not even the destruction by fire of the household refuse which was daily committed to the furnace, to sully the purity of the atmosphere.

I enquired if fires were frequent here, and was told that in the manufacture or adaption of every material in use, either for building purposes, or for decorative and personal application, there was incorporated a substance which rendered it impervious to fire, and practically indestructible.

There was not the slightest noise of traffic in the streets, such as I had always been accustomed to hear in either large or small towns. On each side of every street there was a double means of locomotion provided. Water cars abounded, and by way of proving their comfort and efficiency to me, the two women who escorted me took their seats in one of them, and, somewhat nervously, I followed their example.

In another moment I noticed houses and streets fly past us with magical rapidity, but this phenomenon ceased almost immediately, and I looked through the glass sides of the car upon a totally new scene. Dublin Bay, in all its glorious beauty, lay unfolded to my vision. But I was hardly able to appreciate it at that moment, for I was possessed by the idea that I was under the influence of magic.

The magic subsequently resolved itself into a marvellous adaptation of hydraulic force. It was our car, not the houses, which had been flying with electric speed. Yet so noiseless, and so apparently motionless had we been that the illusion was perfect, and I seemed not to have moved. The pressure of an electric button stopped a car instantaneously, and at the same time prevented any succeeding car from passing a given point until all obstruction ahead was removed.

These stoppages lasted only an infinitesimally short time, for all the cars, whether for passenger or goods traffic, were pulled up to the inner barrier of the double roadway, leaving a clear course for all cars which were still pursuing their journey.

I could not see any water, but was told that the whole traffic of the country was run upon these electric hydraulic ways, and that water had been found so noiseless, so frictionless, so economical, and so superior in every way to the locomotive railways formerly in use as to supersede the latter a few hundred years ago. "Puffing Billy" in fact was now only a memory. The first line of one of Dagonet's ballads, "Billy's dead and gone to glory," came to my mind as applicable to the motive force which in my own days was considered impossible to beat.

His knell was sounded, when there appeared a rival on the scene who brought neither noise, dirt, vibration, nor smoke in her train. Accidents were of almost impossible occurrence on the hydraulic roads, I was told, and ordinary street traffic was not interfered with by these roads, as they were constructed upon elevated platforms.

All persons using them paid a certain sum for the privilege. The State had entire control of the waterways, and derived considerable revenues from them, after paying all expenses, and remunerating the thousands of people who were employed upon them. The remotest part of New Amazonia could, I was told, be reached in twenty minutes, at small cost, as the waterway system scarcely left a village untouched.

I was initiated in many wonders that night, being not the least interested by an inspection of the many strange objects to be seen in the shop windows, and by the universal good humour and happiness which seemed to illumine every face I met. My guides proved themselves to be admirable and patient cicerones. Fortunately for me, they recognised that my physical capabilities were greatly inferior to their own, and did not quite drag me about until I was tired to death.

So far, I was highly satisfied with my adventures in New Amazonia, and when I retired to rest in the luxurious bed provided for me, I slept soundly and healthily until Hilda awoke me, and told me that it was time to get a bath, and dress for breakfast.

ELIZABETH BURGOYNE CORBETT

IX

It could not be more than five o'clock, I was sure, and I did not feel much inclined to rise at such an unconscionably early hour, until I heard Hilda ask if I would not like to go to the large baths with her, and have a swim. Alas! aquatic exercises were utterly out of my power to undertake. But this fact did not deprive me of all desire to witness the doings of others, and I hurriedly left my couch, performed my toilet expeditiously, and accompanied Hilda to the splendid swimming baths in which scores of women were disporting themselves. Their bathing costume was neat and elegant, but at the same time thoroughly utilitarian, and they seemed as much at home in the water as on *terra firma*.

The water was conducted from the sea, and was always cool and fresh, owing to the mechanical arrangements which existed for changing it. I could not help wishing that I could swim, dive, and float like these more favoured beings, but womanfully resisted all attempts to induce me to learn the art there and then.

In all ages, and in all countries, there have been isolated women who have been regarded as beautiful specimens of their sex. In New Amazonia the difficulty would consist in finding women who were not perfect models of beauty, grace, and dignity. As I contemplated the happy groups before me, I had ample opportunity to convince myself that not one of them owed her superb proportions to artificial means, and I was positively thankful that I measured quite twenty-six inches round the waist. Had I measured a fraction less, I should have been looked upon as deformed in this land of goddesses.

I noticed that some of the bathers, not content with simple diving, propelled themselves to a great height by means of trapezes. They would, when at the desired altitude, suddenly relinquish their hold upon the trapeze, turn a somersault, and plunge, straight as a die, into the volume of water beneath. There were many other ways here practised of varying and elaborating these swimming exercises, but no one appeared in the least degree fatigued by them; and I was told that every child was taught swimming from its third year upwards, and that cases of drowning were seldom heard of in this favoured land.

After breakfast, the students repaired to their different classes, and I resolved to venture out alone, my suggestion that I should do so meeting with no opposition.

My want of stature scarcely warranted the assumption that I was a full-grown adult, and the absence of a sash proclaimed me to be of alien race. But I did not doubt now that I should meet with anything but the most courteous treatment. Principal Grey placed a slip of paper in my hand, which proved to be a pass such as the State furnished to all its guests, and was neither more nor less than an open sesame to all public buildings, such as picture galleries and museums. It was also intended to enable me to make such use as I chose of the water-cars.

My first impression that this was a country of none but women had been dissipated on the previous evening by seeing great numbers of men either working or bent upon pleasure. They were magnificent beings, all of them, and presented a superb appearance, such as would have rendered them all-conquering in London society.

Their dress—upon consideration I have decided not to describe their attire. My friend, Mr. Augustus Fitz-Musicus, told me that he meant to produce a book, detailing all his adventures in New Amazonia, and it would hardly be fair to anticipate all he has got to say.

Although I started on my exploring tour with a very good heart, I was not at all sorry when someone presently rushed up to me, and shook my hand with most effusive familiarity. This someone turned out to be Mr. Augustus Fitz-Musicus. He was as much transformed as I was, being dressed in—there now, I nearly betrayed his secret, after all. Considerably to my amusement he professed to be very much disgusted at being compelled to renounce his wonderful tweeds and three-inch high collar, in favour of—well, in favour of garments that were very much more artistic and comfortable.

Like myself, he was thrown upon his own resources for a time, so we resolved to explore in concert, and exchange impressions by the way. Woman has by man been credited with an undying propensity to have the last word on each and every occasion where talking has to be done. My personal conviction is that every man who utters this fallacy knows very well that it is a libel on my sex, and that he is only warding off self-conviction by acting on the principles of first attack.

Thus, Molly Muddle tells Mrs. Bungle that Miss Pringle is too ugly for anything. She has no sooner committed this indiscretion than she becomes afraid that it will be brought home to her, and resolves to preserve her own reputation for charity by straightway informing Miss Pringle that Mrs. Bungle is taking her character away. She repeats and enlarges upon this statement until she actually grows to believe it herself.

It is just so with the men who try to foist their own failings upon women. They are just so many Molly Muddles. Mr. Fitz-Musicus fully bears out this assertion by insisting upon giving me all his experiences before I can get many words in, and by treating me to a repetition of them which lasts until it is time to fulfil our engagements to return in time for the mid-day meal.

"And do you know I am going to write everything down that I see while I am here," he informs me volubly. "Nothing shall escape my notice. In fact, I have begun my book already, for it doesn't do to trust to memory, and as my grasp of the subject is something extraordinary, I expect my book will be no end of a success if I ever go back to the old country."

"Oddly enough," I say, "I have also resolved to publish my impressions of New Amazonia."

"Ah, yes, I daresay," is the supercilious reply. "Of course, there can be no harm in your trying. But you are only a woman, and cannot be expected to produce anything clever. However, I like you, and don't mind touching your work up a bit, before you send it to the printers. In that way, it may possibly be presentable, though of course, it is sure to be rather commonplace. Just listen to my opening paragraph."

Feeling considerably like a cat whose coat is being stroked the wrong way, as I listened to these flattering encomiums on my mental qualifications, I nevertheless paid particular attention to my friend's opening sentences, of which the following is a *verbatim* transcript:—

"The other night, I was with some fellows in London, and we all took some Hasheesh to make us dream. Then I woke up a tree. Then I saw somebody laughing at me, and I came down and tore my trousers. After that, a whole troop of giantesses in queer clothes came and had a look at me. They didn't take any notice of the other party, for she was only a woman. One of the giantesses kissed me, and called me the handsomest fellow she had ever seen. I like that one immensely, and I am seriously thinking of marrying her. I understand that the marriage laws here are just the ticket for rollicking, Bohemian fellows like me. If my wife doesn't prove very obedient and docile, I can chuck her over, and won't even have to keep my own youngsters, if there should be any.

"I don't like the way they house you here. If I stop, I shall insist upon living in a small house, apart from others, where I can make my wife feel that I am lord and master in it.

"The men here seem to be fools. They let the women grow up as strong and healthy as themselves, and it will be difficult to reduce them to civilization again. Isn't it extraordinary?"

This was as far as the rollicking Augustus had progressed in his narrative, and I was quite sincere when I informed him that I thought it very original indeed.

"Oh, I say, you have got your hair cut!" he cried. "It doesn't look at all bad, but when you get back to England you will wish you had it back again. But I suppose you felt that you must be in the fashion. It's a mercy for women that they are at least capable of understanding all matters appertaining to dress. Otherwise, we might expect them to bestow less attention upon our own personal adornment. They can never manufacture anything to equal men's work, but I will grant them the faculty of criticism. How do you like me in my new clothes?"

Should I have been human if I had failed to retaliate a little? On this occasion I found it impossible to resist the temptation, and replied gravely, "Well, Mr. Fitz-Musicus, I confess that I was rather surprised to see that you also had been persuaded to adopt the National costume, for it makes you look more insignificant than ever, if possible. You will be mistaken for some little boy, playing the truant, if you do not mind. But I daresay my presence will be some little protection to you, and you are sincerely welcome to any assistance I can afford you,"—

"Come, if that isn't cool!" interrupted Augustus. "I can see just what is the matter. You are jealous of me all round, because I am naturally of more consequence than you are, and because you have no hope of being able to produce half such a book as mine will be. Still, as I said before, I rather like you, and we may as well be friends while we are here. Suppose we try an intellectual topic likely to prove of use in our reminiscences. What did you have for your breakfast?"

I'm afraid that if I had met Mr. Fitz-Musicus in former days, I should scarcely have looked upon him as an individual with whom it was worth my while to waste ten minutes in conversation, and my chief regret now was that New Amazonians were being edified by the nonentities of a man who was by no means a fair specimen of the sort of men my country could turn out. Not that such conceited individuals do not exist in our midst, for I know someone at this moment who may possibly be mistaken for the prototype of the lively Augustus.

Should he or his friends read this, I wish to assure them that above all things I disclaim being personal. It is not quite an impossibility to find

ELIZABETH BURGOYNE CORBETT

two individuals equally addicted to what is termed fast living; equally boisterous in the matter of dress; equally conceited and overbearing; and addicted to the same inane forms of speech. They may, therefore, console themselves with the idea that, however like them my hero may be, the resemblance is only a chance one.

The further progress of my conversation with the Hon. Augustus would not amuse the reader, anymore than would a description of the remaining portion of that morning's excursion, for I lost all interest in what I saw, and my return to the college took place much earlier than I had intended.

X

The next excursion of any importance which I made was in the company of Principal Grey, who proved a splendid cicerone, inasmuch as she spared no pains to explain everything which presented itself to me in a puzzling aspect. I had often visited different European countries, and had been greatly interested by many things I saw. But in New Amazonia the constant predominating feeling was *amazement*, not mere interest.

Fancy going through a city, anywhere in Europe, in our own days, without seeing either a beggar or a poverty stricken individual of any sort. Dirt, squalor, drunkenness, profane language, sickness, rags, and a thousand other miseries, meet us at every turn in the poorer quarters of our big cities. But not one of these things did I note in New Amazonia. Purity, peace, health, harmony, and comfort reigned in their stead, and presented a picture such as I had never hoped to gaze upon in this world.

But what ultimately struck me as the strangest thing I had yet observed, was the fact that I had not seen a single old woman or man since I came here, and I determined to appease my curiosity on the subject as soon as possible, by addressing some questions to Principal Grey.

"How is it that I have seen no old people since I came to your country?" I asked. "Is it because you keep them secluded after they have arrived at a certain age, or because you die comparatively young?"

"My dear woman," was the Principal's reply, "We have both met and spoken to a great many old people this very evening. Do you mind telling me what you call old age? Perhaps your ideas and mine on the subject differ considerably."

"Well," I replied, "We call seventy or eighty very old, of course."

The Professor looked at me with great astonishment. "Seventy or eighty!" she exclaimed. "Why, how old do you take me to be?"

Had it been an ordinary English lady who had asked me this home question, I should probably have hesitated in my reply. But this was a being who despised the appellative *lady*, with all its accompanying affectations, and prided herself upon nothing so much as being an honest, truthful, candid *woman*. So I made what I considered to be a fair guess, and replied that I judged her age to be about forty or thereabouts.

"Only forty!" was the disparaging comment upon this guess. "I am very glad to say that it is long since I passed that baby age. One must be at least forty-five before a position like mine is attainable. I have occupied my present post for thirty-five years."

"Now, you are asking me to believe too much," I expostulated. "Why, you would at that rate be eighty years old at the very least, and you have not even the suspicion of a wrinkle about you."

"Wrinkles are not necessary evils," I was told. "We prefer to do without them, and seldom see them in real life, though we are familiar enough with their presentment in ancient prints. My actual age is one hundred and fourteen years, and I hope to live a life of honourable usefulness for many years to come, without losing the proud consciousness that I belong to a race of beings fashioned and developed in the Life-giver's own image."

I could only exclaim the surprise I felt at this startling information, and stammer something to the effect that I had never before seen anyone who had lived a whole century, and that when such a rare thing did occur in my country, it was considered a fit occurrence to be recorded in the newspapers.

"Can you tell me what anyone of my age would look like in your country? Supposing that I myself were one of you, and had reached my present age under the normal conditions which govern life with you, what do you really suppose I would look like?"

I am the reverse of clever with my pencil, but the picture which I rapidly sketched would, in my opinion, have proved rather flattering than otherwise, under the circumstances indicated by the Principal. She, however, evidently did not regard it in that light, for she looked at the sketch with a face of horror and repulsion, which was as comical to me as it was evidently real.

"What a frightful country to live in," she exclaimed, "if everyone who has attained to years of discretion is doomed to look like that! I would rather pass my probation with the spirits than endure such a hideous mockery of life. To watch the gradual decay of all physical beauty must be an almost unendurable torment."

"There you are mistaken," I responded, somewhat warmly. "Our old people, provided they have, by an honourable and useful life, gained the respect of their fellows, are honoured more in old age than in comparative youth. It is true that the eyesight becomes impaired; the sense of hearing fails; the teeth fall out; the appetite becomes dulled; strength vanishes; and the gait becomes feeble and halting. But it is also true that in most cases the mental faculties are simultaneously affected, and that the consciousness of physical deterioration, therefore, fails to affect our old people as powerfully as you might think."

"Worse and worse!" cried the Principal, with emphatic conviction. "It seems to me that with you to live is simply to be fully conscious of dying. No New Amazonian would support such a miserable existence for a day. I, for one, would at once resolve to disembody myself, and seek final glorification in a less trammelled state."

"Disembody yourself? Do you mean that you would commit suicide?"

"I mean that my body should cease to live."

"But it is a crime to take the life God gave us."

"I see that superstition ranks rife with you. We should consider it a much greater crime to permit a grovelling, decaying body to chain the spirit to earth and nothingness, than to sever the life which prevents it from seeking perfection in more congenial regions."

"I certainly do feel lamentably dense and ignorant while listening to you. I cannot, for instance, fathom your meaning when you say the spirit can seek perfection after death."

"The spirit never dies. The body is but the casing in which the spirit is given its greatest opportunities of seeking final glorification. As we acquire knowledge of every kind, and learn more and more to fathom the secrets which nature has so long guarded with such jealousy, so much nearer shall we be towards the ultimate perfection of the spirit which assimilates most nearly to Life-giver herself, and constitutes our ideal of final bliss. After the death of our material form, we still strive to reach our desired goal, but our progress, when disembodied, is not so rapid as while still inhabiting our earthly casing, and our ultimate arrival at the zenith of wisdom, purity, and bliss; in other words, Heaven, may be delayed for ages by a premature exit from this world.

"Naturally, therefore, we try to prolong the healthy life of the body by all the arts in our power, knowing that it is given us as a special means of attaining Heavenly perfection. A diseased body inevitably affects the mind, and prevents it from soaring upwards. Therefore, we argue, one of the surest ways of reaching Heaven is to cultivate the health and perfection of the body.

"If this material part of us, therefore, falls into permanent sickness, uselessness, and decay, it but serves to trammel the spirit, and hinder its further advancement. This we are not inclined to tolerate, and when the misfortune of physical wreck overtakes any of us, we liberate the spirit without any wasteful delay. A certain mineral extract, added to an ordinary dose of Schlafstrank, quietly and painlessly disposes of our physical existence, and sends the spirit on its way, rejoicing in its new found freedom."

"You mean that what we call chronic invalidism does not exist among you, simply because your people are in the habit of killing themselves as soon as health leaves them. It is one way of escaping earthly troubles. But are there not some exceedingly painful scenes when the conviction is forced home to anyone that it is becoming necessary to do this? Do you feel no horror of the passage from Here to the great Hereafter?"

"Why should we? A sickly body is no fit tenement for a spirit which is striving for Allwisdom and Deitic Purity. So the sooner we discard it, the sooner we reach Heaven. Sometimes we are sorry to leave friends behind, but I never heard anyone who felt the slightest dread of severance, or who ever hesitated a moment as to the ultimate benefits of such a step. On the contrary, it often occurs that New Amazonians are inclined to discard the body before it is needful or expedient to do so. We, therefore, do not sanction self-extinction until our physicians and surgeons have carefully diagnosed a case, and pronounced their opinion on it. If there is any chance of recovery, the patient is subjected to the influence of Schlafstrank, and eventually awakens cheerfully, prepared to make a sensible use of the respite given to the body. If recovery is hopeless, the patient is provided with mineralized Schlafstrank, and at once cheerfully relinquishes all hold upon matter."

"But suppose the subject is insane; what is done then?"

"Ah, well, insanity is of very rare occurrence with us. The Mother takes such care of her children that they have practically no anxieties. While we are young we are educated and cared for, and when we are old we are always pensioned off, and do not need to labour unless we choose. Few of us, however, care to give up work altogether. When, unfortunately, physical influences work upon the mind in such a manner as to produce the phenomenon called insanity, the Mother at once relieves the spirit of the ties which would effectually prevent the slightest advancement, towards the great goal."

"Kills all insane persons, in fact?"

"Yes; in mercy and justice to themselves."

"And what is your theory as to the condition of insane people after death?"

"Well, they are more remotely removed from the state which entitles us to the bliss of living in unison with Life-giver, because the condition of the body has prevented them from acquiring the degree of perfection which can be reached by healthy persons. But it is only a question of time and degree. Insanity is a disease of the brain; the brain is essentially material; release the spirit from this gross encasement, and its chances of ultimately reaching Heaven are as great as when it first emanated from our glorious Life-giver herself."

"I suppose crime is occasionally to be met with in New Amazonia?"

"Sometimes; but very rarely. There is very little incentive to crime here; when it does occur, we accept it as an indication of a diseased brain, and forthwith use our best efforts to cure the disease. We generally succeed in doing so; but if the case, after repeated and careful doctoring, proves incurable, of course the ordinary treatment of the hopelessly insane is adopted."

"But do you feel no repulsion at the idea of sending a soul stained with crime to Hell?"

"Hell? There is no Hell! That is an old superstition of the Ancients at which I have often wondered."

"After that I am prepared to hear you say that there is no devil!"

"Most certainly I do say so. I have read of the most extraordinary beliefs in witchcraft, sorcery, and the possession by evil spirits, to which all nations used to lend themselves. It was said that they were perpetually at war with all the children of Life-giver, and that the sole purpose of their existence was to prevent people from getting to Heaven. Our great God, whom we call Life-giver, created us in Her image, to be Her associates as soon as our spirits are sufficiently ennobled and purified. Life-giver is good. She has created everything. She loves the creatures She has cast in Her own image. She would not deliberately try to negative Her own work by creating evil spirits to harass us. As for anything being at deliberate war with Her, and going about the world endeavouring to foil Her plans, it is preposterous to believe it. She would at once annihilate anything so monstrous."

"But you surely do not believe that we shall all, good and evil, be awarded the same fate after death?"

"No, I do not. Have I not already tried to explain this to you? Our earthly career is our training school. If we take advantage of all our opportunities, and act in accordance with what we conceive to be the wishes of a Divine and Beneficent Creator, we may hope to be translated to ultimate bliss at no distant period after the death of our bodies. But if we deliberately fail to travel in the direction of steady advancement, we condemn our spirit to endure ages of banishment before it is finally sufficiently purified to partake of the happiness which is the portion of those who have pierced the veil of ignorance, and have entered the kingdom of Divine All-knowledge and Beatitude. You talk of a place called Hell! What worse punishment can be needed for erring souls than to know that to their own perversity they are indebted for being debarred from all happiness and association with purer spirits for ages untold!"

"One more question. We believe that Jesus of Nazareth was sent to save sinners. Do you reject that doctrine?"

"In one sense, yes. In another, no. We believe that from time to time our Creator has permitted individual beings to lead such pure and holy lives as to be a shining example to others, and a stimulus to exertion in the right direction. Jesus of Nazareth was one of the greatest and noblest of these men, and, as such, his name is honoured amongst us. But we do not believe that the Creator awarded incalculable suffering to one creature, in order that we might suffer less. We are sentient beings, and are expected to work out our own salvation."

Thus far Principal Grey had been very patient with me, but as there are limits even to New Amazonian endurance, I resolved to refrain from questioning her further during this walk, and bestowed a little more attention upon surrounding objects, while at the same time carefully weighing the import of our long conversation.

XI

It was not long, however, before my train of thought brought me back to the old groove. I reflected that although I had been told that people whose energies were failing generally preferred to give themselves a quietus, I still did not know how it was that no one seemed to bear any of the usual marks of age. I could hardly believe that the approach of a wrinkle, or a slight failing in any given direction, would be considered a sufficient warning to put an end to earthly troubles and yet I met not a single individual who looked as if she or he was even nearing old age.

"It is strange," I said at last, "that everyone here seems gifted with perpetual youth. I wish you would explain the mystery to me."

"Nothing easier," she rejoined. "I was just taking you to see one of our most important buildings. Follow me."

Nothing loath, and with my curiosity roused to the very apex of expectation, I followed my guide into a magnificent building which we had approached. There were many other people entering at the same time, and more careful observation convinced me that none of them looked quite as bright and healthy as the New Amazonians with whom I had hitherto associated.

I looked enquiringly at Principal Grey. She did but smile, and bid me be seated.

"Wait awhile," she said, "and you shall witness a miracle."

Being deprived of the necessity for action for a time, yet fully appreciating the advantages of a welcome rest, I made diligent use of my eyes, and marvelled much at the rugged, chaste grandeur of the building, which Principal Grey told me was the Andersonia Physiological Hall.

There was a marvellous groined roof, supported by equally marvellous granite pillars. The floor was tesselated, the doors of massive clamped oak, and the windows were wonderful dreams of the glass-painter's art. The splendid staircase which led from the central hall to the upper storys was of brilliant white marble, the balusters being of polished red granite, as were also the numerous fluted columns which supported both staircase and ceiling. The whole building was a perfect dream of taste and splendour, but it was the people, after all, who claimed most of my attention.

It seemed to me that those who entered the Hall, and passed on to what Principal Grey called the "Renewing Rooms," were none of them quite so vigorous and brisk as those who passed us on their return. And yet the latter all seemed to have grown unaccountably stouter in one arm, which they carried with almost wooden stiffness and awkwardness.

Of course I looked my enquiries, but for a time my guide and entertainer preferred to tantalise me by refraining from explaining the mystery which puzzled me.

When at last she did condescend to enlighten my ignorance, I could scarcely restrain my incredulity, for it seemed to me that I was now asked to believe the greatest wonder of all. I was told that the primary purpose of this building was to afford facilities for inoculating the aged or debilitated with the nerves of young and vigorous animals, and that this was the explanation of the fact that I had as yet seen no really old-looking people in New Amazonia.

"We all resort at times to the Physiological Hall for recuperation and rejuvenation," said my companion, "and it is to the benefit we derive here that much of our national prosperity is due. The breeding and rearing of the animals required is an expensive branch of State economy, but all expenses are more than counterbalanced by the fees which we willingly pay for each operation. Even apart from the fact that we are individually and collectively enormously benefitted by our rejuvenating system, it gives employment to a large number of people, and adds considerably to the revenues of the State."

"And since when has the system been in vogue?" I asked, deeply interested.

"Only within the last four hundred years, although it is on reliable record that experiments in that direction were inaugurated by Professor Brown-Sequard in the nineteenth century. But in those days the human race was only just awakening to a knowledge of the benefits and beauties of science, and it remained for posterity to recognise the full value of Professor Brown-Sequard's invention. Do you observe that marble statue, extending the right hand in kindly welcome to all who enter this building?"

"Yes. I noticed it on entering. It is a splendid conception."

"Not more splendid than the genius of the man it is intended to personify. It is a memorial statue of the inventor of Nerve-Rejuvenation. It is essentially idealistic, as no counterfeit presentment of Brown-Sequard has been preserved for the admiration of future ages, but as every statue in his honour is reproduced in the likeness of this one, we are all familiar with what is supposed to be his presentment, just as even in days of old everyone recognised the portrait of Christ the Martyr when they saw it."

I got up to inspect the statue more closely, for I had a sort of second-hand interest in the original. I had once met a gentleman, who had attended his initiatory lecture in Paris on "The Art of not Growing Old." I was sure, however, that the professor would never recognise himself here, for the statue was idealised into the presentment of a beneficent, powerful, godlike form, which was as devoid of all Gallic characteristics, as it was beautiful in conception. I refrained, however, from insinuating that this was the reverse of a true likeness, and contented myself with praising the thing as a work of art.

"And who is your sculptor?" I enquired admiringly.

"Bernard O'Hagan."

"I thought men were excluded from sharing artistic and scientific pursuits with you?"

"By no means. Some of our most famous professors are men and the Lectureships are open to all who can head the list in our annual competitions. The chief Governmental offices are all appropriated by women, in sheer self-defence, in the first instance, and, later on, because the world's experience goes to prove that masculine government has always held openings for the free admission of corruption, injustice, immorality, and narrow-minded, self-glorifying bigotry. The purity and wisdom of New Amazonian Government is proverbial, and we know better than to admit the possibility of retrogression by permitting male governance again. Nevertheless, we are not disposed to be narrow-minded ourselves, by way of avenging past oppression. Our Tribunes, Privy Councillors, Prime Advisers, and Leader are always women. But with respect to everything else, the sexes stand on an equal footing, both women and men who have attained the age of forty-five being privileged to vote at all elections."

"And in the case of married people, which is supposed to be the head of the household?"

"Whichever of the two happens to be best qualified to direct domestic affairs with the greatest wisdom. Our tenets preach equality in the married state, and as people of uncongenial temperament have no trouble in obtaining a divorce, it is seldom that serious marital disturbances are heard of. The mere knowledge that marriage is a civil compact, which may almost be dissolved at will, serves to restrain violent ebullitions of temper. As a rule, our divorcees are very good friends after their marriage has been judicially dissolved."

ELIZABETH BURGOYNE CORBETT

"Still, domestic involvements of this sort must serve to distract the attention from serious duties, and reduce individual capability of taking an active part in public work."

"Your deduction is perfectly logical, but has no foundation in fact, for this reason—we permit no one to be elected for State offices who has ever been married; nor are important professorial posts accessible by them, although trade agencies and countless minor offices are open to them. The result of this policy is manifold. Our population scarcely increases at all, and the necessity of emigration, which is practised by less moral and more prolific nations, does not even loom in the distant future for us. We have no great dearth of resources to face, nor have we to battle with the incalculable evils forced upon other States by over-population. Our laws and social economy hold out wonderful premiums for chastity, and the result is that all our most intellectual compatriots, especially the women, prefer honour and advancement to the more animal pleasures of marriage and re-production of species."

"Am I to understand from this, that you do not hold the condition of motherhood in honour?"

"By no means. If you will take careful note of your surroundings ere you leave us, you will see that as much public homage is paid to married women as to single ones. But we believe that perfect clearness of brain, and the ability to devote oneself exclusively to intellectual topics, are inseparable from the celibate state, and we adhere rigidly to the rules established in connection with this subject."

"It must, I suppose, be impossible even here to escape some taint of immorality. For instance, it must be a great temptation to many people to keep themselves eligible for election by remaining single, and yet to indulge secretly in carnal propensities. How do you act in the case of illegitimate children?"

"Illegitimate children are an almost unheard of phenomenon here. We do not tolerate vice, and our punishments usually prove adequate deterrents. A woman found guilty of adultery is at once degraded, and never attains to any other position than that of the lowest menial in one of our public institutions."

"And what of the man? He is allowed to go scot-free with us. Is it so with you?"

"No man who has once offended in that direction ever has the opportunity of repeating his crime in New Amazonia, for he is at once bereft of all he possesses, and banished from the country. Not only does he lose all present possessions, but forfeits the pension he would otherwise enjoy in his old age. He is not permitted to return to the country."

"Then your punishment of the man is infinitely the most severe?"

"Yes. It is long since we recognised the necessity of repressing vice by other methods than our forerunners adopted."

"And what are your laws in relation to the legal and moral rights of illegitimates?"

"We have no laws on the subject, simply because the offspring of vice is not permitted to live. We New Amazonians pride ourselves upon being of none but honourable parentage."

This information was delivered in such a calm and matter-of-fact tone that I involuntarily shuddered, and hastened to change the subject.

"Do you think I could witness an operation in that inner room without feeling specially horrified?" I asked next.

"You shall yourself be operated upon, if you will," replied Principal Grey. "You are a guest of the Mother, and will have no fees to pay, but you will derive wonderful benefit. I wish to be operated upon myself, and we will go in together."

"But stay one moment. Did you not say that people were inoculated at the expense of young animals, whose nerves are used to rejuvenate their tormentors? I cannot possibly go in there, and face vivisectional cruelties. To see the poor brutes writhe in tortured agony; to witness the fearful rolling of their glaring eyeballs; to listen to their despairing cries and groans, in order that I may benefit by their sufferings, is an ordeal I cannot go through. I will wait here, until you have been inoculated, but I cannot go myself."

"Nonsense, my dear woman," smiled the Principal. "You are talking with no more perception of the advancement of science than if you really lived in that nineteenth century to which you so oddly claim to belong. The animals do not suffer one little bit, as you will see when you go into the 'Renewing Rooms.' Long ago, a German chemist invented a wonderful ether, which he called 'Bändiger.' It had the power of instantaneously arresting sense and motion. Perfect unconsciousness was produced with electrical rapidity, and the clever chemist expected to earn his country's gratitude for his marvellous discovery. But in those days governments were exceedingly narrow-minded, and the German Government was so struck with the remarkable powers for harm which the new discovery possessed, that it ignored all its beneficial qualities,

ELIZABETH BURGOYNE CORBETT

and actually forbade the chemist to manufacture 'Bändiger' in future. Happily, he was more enlightened than his rulers, and not merely did his best to improve upon his invention, but left careful instructions to his successors relating to its manufacture. Many years after this, a miniature revolver was invented which, instead of cartridges, was charged with minute cells of 'Bändiger.' These 'Bändiger' revolvers were subsequently manufactured in large quantities in America, and as the State monopolised the manufacture, and charged high prices for every weapon, besides exacting a heavy tax for the privilege of using them, they proved a very profitable monopoly. From America their use spread to India, where they were speedily efficacious in ridding the country of the countless numbers of wild beasts which annually slaughtered a great proportion of the population. The 'Bändiger' does not kill. It only stuns instantaneously, the effect lasting long enough to enable us to kill outright, or to make such experiments as are required in the interests of science and progress. An animal once subjected to its influence feels no more pain, for it is absolutely unconscious during all subsequent operations, and if it has been too much cut up to recover easily, it is at once killed. If not, the administration of Schlafstrank enables it to recuperate painlessly, and be available for future experiments."

"This 'Bändiger' is really a frightful power. Does it never happen that crime is committed by its aid?"

"Never. Nobody ever has the handling of a 'Bändiger' revolver, except our duly qualified and licensed surgeons, and they would not imperil their future existence and prosperity by stupid indulgence in a senseless freak. But come, we must now go in, or the rooms will be closed for the day."

This time I was not reluctant to follow the Principal, and I was very agreeably surprised on entering the "Renewing Room." My mind's eye had conjured a vision of gory disorder, the central figure of which was the quivering and bleeding body of some unhappy animal, and the prominent accessories some brawny and bare-armed surgeons, whose perspiring brows, blood-stained hands, and callous cruelty of expression would be anything but reassuring to the trembling and expectant human beings waiting to be inoculated.

What I really saw was this: The room to which an attendant conducted us was richly carpeted, and furnished with Oriental luxuriousness. Every accessory to comfort was there, and several people were either standing talking in animated groups, or lounging on the spacious cushioned chairs and settees. Some were reading, some sipping coffee, some playing with some beautiful dogs, that basked in front of the fire. A few were busy at needlework, but all seemed thoroughly at home. There were several tables laden with prints and papers. A magnificent bookcase occupied one end of the room. The walls were panelled in bird's-eye maple, and decorated with beautiful pictures, all photographed in their natural colours, which stood out as vivid and brilliant as in an oil painting.

The operating surgeons were six in number—four of them being women, two men. They were all handsome, of splendid physique, elegantly dressed, and of dignified yet gentle and calm demeanour. Not a bit like the ogres my excited fancy had pictured.

In one of the window recesses was a sort of bassinette, in which a large dog lay motionless, and apparently sleeping, with a screen partially hiding him from observation. To this dog the surgeons journeyed before attacking the bared arm of the individual to be operated upon. In an incredibly short time the task of inoculation was performed, the people hardly ceasing their pleasant hum of conversation the while. Then the arm was tightly bandaged, and the patient went on her or his way rejoicing, after paying the necessary fees to an official whose duty it was to receive them in an ante-room.

Presently an electric-bell was rung. Two attendants entered the room, pushed the bassinette through a door at one side of the window, and drew an empty one from an opening at the other side. Then one of the dogs was coaxed from the hearth, and given a dainty and appetising meal, afterwards springing upon the bassinette to enjoy a quiet nap after his good dinner. In another second the "Bändiger" had done its work, and in a few minutes more some of the dog's nerve force was being transferred to my own arm.

The sensation I experienced was little more than a pinprick in intensity, but, before I left the building with Principal Grey, I felt ten years younger and stronger, and was proportionately elated at my good fortune.

XII

A subsequent conversation I had with Principal Grey also struck me as so noteworthy that I jotted the particulars of it down without delay, for the benefit of possible future English readers.

I had observed that although there were plenty of people dressed with distinctive badges and colours, whose function it was to preserve order and regulate the traffic, as the policemen do with us, I saw none whom I could assume to be soldiers, and made enquiries on the subject. I was told that standing armies were seldom maintained now, as it was no longer the custom of nations to decimate each other by public slaughter, but to trust to a system of international arbitration in the event of quarrels arising.

Nevertheless, as New Amazonia was a temptingly wealthy State, thanks to its perfect financial organisation, there was a possibility of invasion, and great care had been lavished upon its fortifications, which, when manned, or womaned, with trained warriors, were all but impregnable.

"Then," I said, "you do possess a trained army, after all?"

"In one sense, yes. But not in the sense you mean. We are all trained to fight, and there is not a woman or man in the country who does not thoroughly understand military discipline. Our training begins in infancy, and includes riding, shooting, swimming, diving, ballooning, and every possible military exercise. In time of war we should all receive remuneration commensurate with what we realise by the aid of our ordinary avocations, *plus* an additional third. Our discipline is severe, but we glory in it, and all New Amazonia could be ready for action within an hour. A few foolhardy attempts to vanquish us have been made, but our foes suffered so severely that we are scarcely likely to be molested again. Still, our vigilance is never relaxed, and our cordon of sentries is so perfect and efficient, that not even one stranger can intrude here without being speedily discovered. These sentries perform a double duty, for they effectually prevent all attempts to either import or export any goods that have not yielded their due proportion of profit to the Mother."

"Then New Amazonians cannot claim exemption from the temptation to smuggle?"

"No, and yes. Such attempts used to be frequent in bygone days, but the punishment for smuggling is so severe, and immunity from detection so problematical, that the vice is almost stamped out."

"And what is the punishment meted to offenders in this direction?"

"Foreigners are publicly whipped and expelled, *minus* their goods. New Amazonians are deprived of civil rights and relegated to inferior duties."

"Bad enough," I soliloquised. "And, now, there is another thing which puzzles me somewhat. What with war, seafaring, and a thousand accidents to which men are more exposed than women, so many male lives are lost in my country, that the feminine element predominates everywhere, just as it seems to have done in Teuto-Scotland, when the project of re-colonising Ireland was first mooted. Is there a tendency in this direction with you now? And, if so, do you take steps to counteract it?"

"We have devoted much thought to the subject; and have come to the conclusion that even where all the causes of masculine extinction which you have named are absent, then is still a tendency for women to outnumber men. This is easily accounted for. Very few children die with us in infancy, but it is a fact that boys succumb more easily to infantile disorders than girls. We desire to preserve an equality of the sexes, nevertheless, and perfect physiological knowledge enables us to solve this problem, as we have done many others which the Ancients deemed unsolvable."

"I notice that all your people are magnificently formed, but you must be subject to certain ailments. Toothache, for instance, which is a perfect scourge with us."

"That is a phenomenon to which we are here quite strange, I am glad to say. We would as soon expect our skulls to become diseased, as to see our teeth decay. We know the exact chemical constituents of bone, and are careful to supply the constitution with perfect bone-forming food. We also avoid everything that has been proved to be an injurious article of diet."

"But individual temptation must sometimes break through this rule of abstinence?"

"It cannot. No sooner is anything condemned by the Mother, than its importation or manufacture is strictly forbidden, and that particular article is soon unobtainable in the country."

"I suppose malformed or crippled children are occasionally brought into the world, even here. What becomes of them?"

"They are at once sent to spend their term of probation in less material spheres."

"Now, in relation to love matters. With which sex rests the onus of proposing marriage?"

"With either sex, of course I do not see how it could be otherwise."

"It is very much otherwise with us. A woman may be dying for love, but she is not supposed to betray the fact to anyone, until the object of her desires intimates that he has set his affections upon her."

"But suppose that he intimates no such thing? Do you mean to say that she is not even then to express her preference?"

"Then less than ever! The object of her affections would not think her worth having if she were won too easily, even if he wanted her. If he did not want her, he would most probably sneer about her love-lorn condition to all his acquaintances, and they would be highly amused at her unwomanliness in presuming to love before she had been asked."

"Well, I do not envy you your social institutions! It seems to me that your men must be insufferable cads, and your women nothing less than fools. Why do they permit such an anomalous state of things? Can they not see that this is only another of the countless meshes with which masculine egotism has woven the net of slavery and oppression? The man who can look upon a true woman's love for himself with anything but respect and grateful sympathy is nothing better than a cur, who is himself unworthy of the esteem of all honourable people."

The Principal spoke with considerable warmth, and I was so struck with the force of her remarks, that I promised to lay her views before my own countrywomen at no distant date. I had, however, not much confidence in the efficacy of any appeal I might make to womanly pride, seeing that so little has yet been done in England to induce women to think and act for themselves, and to endeavour to break through the multitude of social barriers which have been erected by man's selfishness, tyranny, and arrogance. Still, it has often happened that the absurdity of a custom has only needed to be demonstrated in black and white for its doom to be sealed, and I introduce this subject to the notice of my countrywomen, in the hope that it may induce some of them to bestow a little more thought upon the anomalies of their position, and use their best endeavours to remove at least some of the partially self-created disabilities they suffer from.

By way of diverting the Principal's attention from a subject which aroused both her anger and contempt, I remarked upon the delightful purity of the atmosphere here, and opined that infectious diseases could not be very prevalent.

"We have heard of such evils," was the reply, "but science and common sense united have combated them effectually. Two of our finest statues are in honour of a couple of scientists who must be ranked amongst the most famous benefactors of their kind who have ever lived. I allude to Koch and Pasteur, whose discoveries inaugurated a happy era of immunity from disorders which once killed thousands of human beings annually. Unfortunately for their contemporaries, the world at large looked upon their discoveries as only interesting from the scientists' point of view, failing to recognise the fact that a gigantic revolution in medicine was impending. In some of our archives mention is made of a Dr. Austin Flint, who asserted that such a revolution was not far off. But his utterances fell on ears that were mostly deaf or unheeding. And yet, to the discovery and study of bacteria the most incalculable benefits to the human race are to be attributed. So perfect has the knowledge on this subject now become, that the cause of every infectious disease is well known. They are all easily preventible, but where, through possible slight relaxation of watchfulness, they may break out, they are so easily curable as to cause no alarm. It is, however, many years since a case of infectious disease occurred in New Amazonia. Science has succeeded in affording us absolute protection against scarlet fever, measles, yellow fever, cholera, whooping cough, and many other dreadful ailments which formerly decimated nations."

Naturally, I was very much interested in all these statements, and our conversation branched into various departments of the curative art. I was considerably amused by Principal Grey's information relative to the Dietetic Hospital, as fine a building as any I had yet noticed in Andersonia.

The patients in this hospital were nearly all people in physical health, and they pursued their ordinary daily avocations with a cheerfulness which I had never before observed in an institution patronised solely for its curative properties. The Dietists, as they were called, resorted to this hospital in search of cures for mental and moral failings, and implicitly obeyed the specialists who sought to effect their cure by means of a wise and judicious selection of food.

Thus the violent tempered found their nature considerably modified and sweetened, after being for a few months subjected to a daily diet in which a peculiarly prepared carrot-soup was the *pièce de résistance*. Nervous disorders were very few here, but the slightest suspicion of a tendency to be nervous or fidgety was provocative of a temporary flight to the hospital, which, owing to the speed and cheapness of the water-cars, was easily accessible to every denizen of the island. Green peas and

ELIZABETH BURGOYNE CORBETT

scarlet runners were prohibited to those whose natural tendencies ran in a choleric direction, since they were held to be provocative of violent temper.

On the other hand, dried peas and lentils were high in favour, as they were said to impart good humour. The fat and frivolous were dieted partially on turnips, in order to curtail their physical tendency to ponderosity, and their mental leaning towards superabundance of spirits. To cabbage a thousand virtues were ascribed, and the idea that the consumption of animal food produced coarseness of mind and body was responsible in great measure for the disgust with which the foreign habit of flesh-eating was regarded.

Knowing what I now did of the peculiar religious beliefs of New Amazonians, I could easily conceive that the most scrupulous attention would be paid to dietetic and sanitary matters, since a healthy body was supposed to facilitate the perfecting of the spirit, and its final glorification.

The importance attached to diet and sanitation reminded me forcibly of the old Mosaic laws, and I enquired if great importance was attached to the Testamentary records of Ancient History handed down to us in the Bible.

"Certainly," replied the Principal, very emphatically, "but we also heed Herodotus and Josephus; and our greatest classical work on ancient history has been compiled by twelve New Amazonian savants, who compared all come-at-able records with such strict impartiality and absence of special bias, that we flatter ourselves upon possessing the most accurate and reliable records of ancient history extant."

"But you surely reverence the Bible?"

"Yes, we reverence it, most assuredly. But where historical accuracy seems to be slightly at fault, we are not above being instructed from other sources."

"Then what do you think of Moses as a historian, as a law-giver, and as a general?"

"In all these respects we think that he was truly great. But, being human, it was not impossible for him to adopt an erroneous opinion on a given subject, or to commit a grave error of judgment. Many things for which we can now find natural explanations must have seemed miraculous in his days, and in no case do we believe that he placed anything on record which he did not believe to be exactly as he described it. Still, this does not prevent us from recognising some errors in his accounts of the doings in former times. That he forsook the precincts of a Court, in order to cast in his lot with his own downtrodden and oppressed people, is proof sufficient of his innate nobility, and his fearless defence of the ill-treated Israelitish labourers showed that he had also plenty of the courage required in a great leader."

"And what of David?"

"King David does not arouse my personal estimation. He attained to great eminence, and founded a family which boasted as its scion Christ the Martyr himself. He also wrote some beautiful poetry. But when it comes to an analysis of private character, he does not shine greatly. Naturally, however, the Jews, whose national prestige he increased so materially, think very highly of him. Upon the whole, we prefer the New Testament to the Old, for the sake of its beautiful moral teachings, as well as for its historical importance."

"You do not adhere to all its commandments?"

"No, it would be ill for us if we did. Never to speak in an assembly; to be compelled to carry a great weight of hair about with us; to be subservient to men in all things, and to foster woman's disabilities and man's arrogance, to the extent preached by some of the Apostles, is repugnant to the common sense of every woman who is able to think for herself. But when we come across anything that is offensive to our self-respect, we make due allowances for the egotism of man and the customs of the times. We also remember that Jesus always showed Himself to be woman's true friend and associate; in fact, Jesus is the one pure and shining light which the world has produced, of whom it can truly be said that He was free from all trace of egotism, bigotry, and arrogance. His every word and action bespoke the possession of that Divine charity which thinketh no evil. No wonder that even yet He is by many regarded as God himself. Surely His spirit would pass to eternal glory without any of the probation which we expect to endure before we reach the perfection which shall entitle us to dwell in the uttermost realms of bliss."

"And yet there must be many beautiful natures in so happy a land as this."

"I grant it. But the nature that can avoid sullying the soul with wrongdoing in these enlightened days cannot compare with the purity and goodness of a soul which walked unstained through life in the days of bigotry, superstition, and ignorance."

"That is true. But if we accept this opinion, we must also accept its natural correlative, and consider that the sinner of today is more blameworthy than those who sinned when to be good was not so easy as it is now."

"Few will dispute that point with you. But it becomes necessary for me to remind you now that unpunctuality, and neglect of duty, are grave sins with us. You will, therefore, excuse me for a time, since it becomes necessary for me to address the students in a few minutes from now."

I felt rebuked for my presumption in encroaching so much upon the Principal's time. But she was so very good-natured, and so exceedingly willing to gratify my curiosity, that I was tempted to trespass upon her indulgence, being urged thereto by a sense of unreality, and a conviction that my stay in New Amazonia would terminate as suddenly and as mysteriously as it had begun. It was natural, therefore, that I should wish to post myself up in all the information obtainable during my sojourn here.

XIII

A few hours later, I was honoured by a most embarrassing request. I say honoured, because the request was the outcome of a desire to pay due attention to a visitor who possessed a good passport to New Amazonian favour in that she took an intelligent interest in her surroundings. If I add that my diminutive stature, curious appearance, and mysterious mode of arrival had somewhat tickled the national vein of curiosity, I shall not be far wrong.

The service required of me was to make a public speech, in which I was asked to give a slight account of the manners and customs of my own country, as well as the best explanation I could give of my journey hither, and my mode of eluding the coastguard. No doubt many of my readers may think that such a request would not have embarrassed them. They could have talked glibly enough, and would have felt quite comfortable when addressing the audience which intended to listen to my feeble utterances.

As for giving a succinct account of the journey, they could have invented on the spot so marvellous a recital as would have excited the wonderment of every New Amazonian. I am quite willing to admit that to these clever individuals the forthcoming meeting would have presented no terrors. But they may possibly comprehend my feelings when I tell them that I had never lectured, or made a speech before a large audience in my life. And yet, here was I expected to pose my insignificant self upon a public platform, and address a crowded meeting at an hour's notice, conscious all the time that thousands of people were criticising my odd appearance and old-fashioned diction.

It certainly was no small ordeal for me to face, and I am not at all sure that my trepidation was lessened by the information that the Honourable Augustus was also going to give a recital of his adventures. To be honest, I was not proud of his ability, and I was rather afraid lest he should allow himself to be carried away by his insular, as well as by his masculine conceit, and bring ridicule upon both of us. For, although we knew nothing of each other's antecedents, it was inevitable that we should be coupled together in the minds of New Amazonians, who had never met with our like before.

Myra was solicitous that I should look my very best, and save for the sash, which aliens were not permitted to wear, I was as gay as any

ELIZABETH BURGOYNE CORBETT

unofficial native who would be present. My escort was a large one. It seemed to me that all the college was going, and long before we entered the magnificent Hall of Discussion, in which I was to pose as one of the central figures, I had come to the conclusion that everybody else in Andersonia was bound for the same place.

"I do believe that the Hall is going to prove too small tonight," remarked Myra, as we gained the entrance, where a large crowd was endeavouring to obtain an early turn at the automatic gate which permitted none but presentees of a certain coin of the realm to obtain access to the auditorium.

Myself and escort passed up a grand staircase, and presently reached the platform, where my own appearance proved the signal for a loud and long-continued burst of applause, which was presently renewed when Mr. Fitz-Musicus was ushered on to the platform.

He wasn't nervous. I could see that at a glance. I never saw anyone look around on a vast multitude of people with such a superlatively ridiculous affectation of arrogance and accentuated self-esteem, and a curious conviction suddenly assailed me. The Honourable Augustus was not of the sort of material that can ever be brought to eat humble pie, under any circumstances whatever. His experiences in this marvellous country only served to emphasize his national prejudices, and I could see that, so far from acknowledging native superiority, he was bent upon making the erstwhile proud boast that he was "a true born Englishman."

A quick, compassionate glance which he threw at me also revealed the fact that he rather pitied me for the feminine ignorance and incompetence which I was doomed to display ere long. But, somehow, the irritation which his presence invariably aroused in me dispelled the feeling of tremour with which I had hitherto been possessed, and I defiantly resolved that whatever Mr. Fitz-Musicus himself might think upon the subject, our audience should not vote my oratorical powers so vastly inferior to his.

My sojourn in New Amazonia had already tended to bestow more vigour upon me, and since my visit to the Renewing Rooms I had felt unwontedly strong. Now that pique, wounded vanity, or a natural spirit of emulation—call it what you will—had banished my nervousness, I felt equal to any demands which were likely to be made upon my powers of endurance. The Honourable Augustus was also somewhat improved in physique, but I did not fear the contest, as I instinctively felt that the very weapons with which he was so fond of asserting his superiority to my own unfortunate sex would be the means of his undoing in popular esteem, if brought into action on this occasion.

The proceedings began by our introduction to several prominent New Amazonian celebrities, one of whom was no less an individual than the Leader herself, whose dark green velvet attire was so richly embroidered with gold tissue that she looked perfectly resplendent. Her cap and sash were, in addition, adorned with gems, of which the prevailing design was a harp encircled with shamrocks, the harps being outlined in diamonds, and the shamrocks in emeralds.

The Leader herself was a magnificent woman, who, when her term of office expired, would once more lapse into her former condition of comparative obscurity as Professor of Moral Philosophy, for it was one of the laws of this strange land, that whenever a Leader's term of office had run out, she should for ten years at least take no further active part in the government of her country. The next Leader elected was always one of the Prime Advisers, who had already done duty in the ranks of the Privy Councillors, these in their turn being elected by popular vote from the Tribunes. It was considered desirable to afford equal chances to every candidate for Office, hence the limitations of time insisted upon.

When the Leader entered, the whole audience rose to greet her. Then, as soon as she and her escort were seated, and our introduction to her was graciously acknowledged, Principal Grey, in a few well-chosen words, described how one of her students had encountered the two strangers in the college garden, and the arrangements that had been made for our comfort and entertainment.

While she was still speaking, the Honourable Augustus skipped over the stage on tiptoe and enquired *sotto voce*, "I say, are you going to speak first, or am I?"

"Just as you like," I replied in a whisper, willing to do anything to get rid of him, and cover his breach of manners in creating a diversion while Principal Grey was still speaking.

"That's all right, then," he exclaimed, evidently greatly relieved. "You see, I am used to speaking in public; and you are not. You might spoil the impression I wish to create, if you spoke first. And besides—"

"For goodness sake bestow your attention upon your surroundings," I interrupted hurriedly, standing up as I spoke, and accepting the hand of Principal Grey, who led me forward, and introduced me to the audience, a very handsome man performing the like service for the Honourable Augustus, who bowed so theatrically, and looked so killingly dudish, that the one prevailing expression on the faces of all who saw him was a large smile, which produced radiant satisfaction in Augustus.

"Mr. Fitz-Musicus wishes to speak first," I quietly informed the Principal. She looked not a little surprised at what she evidently regarded as his presumption. But no objection was made to the proposal, and in another moment we were listening to the Honourable Augustus's remarkable peroration.

"Ladies and gentlemen," he began, and was forthwith astounded to hear deprecating murmurs all over the house. For an instant he looked dumbfounded, then he seemed to think he knew what was wrong, and recovered his presence of mind with magical swiftness. "I beg the pardon of all those here assembled," he continued, "I ought to have said *gentlemen* and *ladies*. We are more polite in our country, and always, when in public, do our best to flatter the *inferior sex*. However, since you prefer it the other way, here goes. It is with great pleasure, gentlemen and ladies—"

But it was quite impossible to catch what he said next, for he had tickled the national sense of humour, and though the individual laughter of each one present was the gentlest possible expression of New Amazonian merriment, the collective result quite deadened the sound of the "distinguished stranger's" voice.

At this juncture the Speaker rose to her feet, and stepped to the side of the Honourable Augustus. In an instant the deepest silence reigned, as all listened for the words of wisdom which were expected to fall from her lips.

"My children," she began gravely, her rich voice filling the Hall with melodious sound, "must I remind you that the laws of hospitality are violated when the slightest interruption of the evening's programme is made? Do you forget that it was well-known ere we met this evening that our guests have been brought up under conditions so dissimilar to our own, that it is impossible for them to be acquainted with our usual forms of address, I must crave your strict silence during the remainder of the proceedings. And you, Mr. Fitz-Musicus," she continued, "will perhaps pardon me if I here offer the information that neither 'ladies' nor 'gentlemen' are supposed to exist in New Amazonia. We pride ourselves upon being honest, matter-of-fact 'women' and 'men,' and discard the other appellations as too suggestive of affectations and mannerisms. You will, therefore, kindly excuse the feeling of surprise with which most of us heard ourselves greeted by words which, with us, are terms of opprobrium."

While she spoke, the Honourable Augustus stood looking at her with an expression of jaunty ease which spoke volumes for the invulnerability of his *sang froid*, and even induced me to look at him with feelings in which admiration fought for a place on a plane with my amusement.

"Oh, don't mention it, madam," he said, airily, "I might have known that you did not aspire to the same level of culture as the English. All the same, I am very glad if I can afford you amusement, so here goes once more."

Raising his voice, he now turned to the audience, and so perfect were the acoustic properties of the Hall, that every word he uttered was heard in the most distant corner.

"I suppose," he said coolly, "that I may safely take your Mrs. Leader as my model, and address you as 'My children.' Mighty big children some of you are, too. I can't help thinking that I wouldn't like too many of your size to provide for. But although it is a common adage in good old England that, 'good stuff is put into little compass,' I am willing to admit that there may be exceptions, and I honestly think that the Irish race has improved since I first knew it. But you are not here to listen to my opinions of you, but to hear my explanation of the reasons and the method which brought me hither.

"Our parsons—I suppose you have parsons here, too—as I said, our parsons always divide their sermons under several heads. I will be more considerate, and use only two. In the first place, I am not conscious of ever having had any reasons for coming here. In the second place, I know no more of the method in which I journeyed hither than the man in the moon. You seem to have abolished a good many things here, but I don't suppose you have abolished the man in the moon, so you will know what I mean. Still, I believe I can offer some sort of explanation that will be of interest to my audience.

"When at home in my native country, I am thought pretty well of by those who know me. In fact, I may say that I am rather a favourite both with my own and the fair sex. This is all very well in some respects, but is not exactly an unmixed advantage. It may not be generally known here that I am entitled to wear the Royal Arms with a bar sinister, one of my ancestors being no less a personage than a King of England, whom it behoved to provide for his offspring, since his benighted people showed a disinclination to do so.

"Unfortunately, the splendid title and pension bestowed upon the progenitress of our family honours and emoluments have been appropriated by my elder brother, the Duke of Quaverly, and my own allowance is so small as to be totally inadequate to the needs of a scion of a noble house. This has caused the limits of my enjoyments to be somewhat circumscribed, but there is one means of increasing my pleasures which never fails me. The practice to which I allude may not be known to you foreigners, but you have reason to thank it, for to it you owe the opportunity of listening to a speech by the Honourable Augustus Fitz-Musicus.

"I cannot say how long it is since, for I have got rather mixed up in my dates. But one evening I accompanied a friend of mine to a certain establishment in Soho, where we partook of some Hasheesh, and, comfortably reclining upon some velvet lounges, resigned ourselves to the enjoyment of the dreams which we expected. My dreamy state came on soon enough, but the first thing I remember is finding myself stuck up an apple tree. I must leave it to the perspicacity of the assembled multitude to explain how I came there.

"As you already know, I was not the only fresh importation from my country, but the other party will speak for herself by-and-bye. Then one of your—a—must I say women? Ah, yes—one of your women, and a dooced fine woman too, came upon the scene; cut the other party altogether; took a violent fancy to myself; and informed others of my arrival. I have been well-treated since I came here, that is, as well as you know how to do it.

"But I think it's a confounded nuisance not to be able to get hold of a bit of butcher's meat. And it's just beastly to be unable to raise a smoke in any shape or form.

"There are many other things in which we Londoners at least can beat you into fits. There is a much greater proportion of married women among us. I have been told that the women here prefer to be old maids, but I know a trick worth two of that. I have often heard the same sort of thing in England, and the very people that professed such sentiments always snapped at the first chance of a husband they got, I may say that I prefer teetotalism just now, but oh, Jemima! don't I wish that some of you would tempt me with a bottle of Moët and Chandon! In fact, the very thought of all I am deprived of while here has thoroughly upset me, and I don't care how soon I'm home again."

Saying this, poor ill-used Augustus ceased speaking, and sat down on the seat provided for him with such a sour and discontented expression on his face that one could almost fancy a transformation had taken place, and that was someone other than the man who commenced his speech so jauntily.

As for the audience, it seemed to me that every face I looked at wore an expression of disgust at the man who was rewarding the Mother's hospitality so rudely. The deep silence which followed upon the speech from which much edification had been expected, appeared to me to be so ominous of displeasure, that all my erstwhile nervousness re-appeared in full force.

But I was anxious to undo the unpleasant impression which my countryman had made, and, the initiatory sentence of my speech once got over, I talked fluently enough. I really do not remember half of what I said, but think that I must have expressed myself graphically and satisfactorily enough, for I sat down amid a perfect thunder of applause, which caused the Honourable Augustus to look daggers at me. I daresay he was justified in doing so, for I fancy that when I was drawing comparisons between my own country and the one in which we were sojourning, and all to the credit of the latter, he believed me to be actuated more by a desire to flatter my audience than to speak the honest truth.

That he was mistaken in this respect I can truthfully say, but I do not suppose he has forgiven me to this day, unless he has come to look upon the whole affair as the production of his Hasheesh-laden imagination. But whatever my countryman may have thought of my performance, it evidently satisfied everybody else, and I was very glad that this was so, as I felt that some return was due from me for all the kindness and hospitality I had met with during my sojourn here.

XIV

I was now invited as the guest of many distinguished personages, and thoroughly enjoyed my life for the next few days. I found New Amazonian men quite as charming as the women, both as regards physique and culture. Beards were in great favour here, and shaving was decidedly at a discount, but a great length of hair was not coveted by anyone, and the beards were always neatly clipped.

At the different entertainments I noticed a great deal of promiscuity such as would hardly be tolerated in aristocratic English society. Not that there was ever anyone present who was not perfectly well-bred. But intellect was the principal passport to social privileges here, and we all know that intellectuality may languish in obscure corners in England, unless backed by strong personal or monetary interest, and that our class prejudices are unpleasantly strong.

A young mechanician whom I met at the house of one of the Prime Advisers was a universal favourite, and his modesty and good sense were admirable foils to the plethora of self-esteem which I have seen engendered in English "lions" for far less potent reasons. I was told that his inventions and improvements in matters relating to sanitary science were so marvellous and of so beneficent a nature, that he was to be rewarded with the medal of the Order of Merit, an honour which, it will be observed, was well worth having, he being only the thirtieth recipient within two hundred years.

It was not difficult for me to secure an interview with him, as mutual curiosity drew us together. If I had expected his conversation to savour of "shop," I was strongly mistaken, for not a word of his own great achievements did he breathe, and he drew me out so skilfully, that half-an-hour passed in conversation with him before his professional instincts were at all aroused, and then it was in response to some reply I had made respecting the locality in which I resided when last I remembered being in my own country.

"Within fifteen minutes walk of the house in which George Stephenson resided!" he exclaimed in great wonderment. "I always understood that it was quite a humble affair. Surely it must have crumbled to dust centuries ago?"

"By no means." I returned. "The cottage looked very pretty and picturesque the last time I saw it. It is tenanted by people who take a pride in the garden, and it would compare favourably in external appearance with any other cottage of the same size in England. It is known locally as the 'Dial House,' as it boasts a sundial of which some portion was the work of Stephenson himself. At the end of the house is a very well-stocked greenhouse, and the space of ground in which the great engineer had some lines laid for experimental purposes is converted into a kitchen garden."

"It seems so incredible, that I can hardly take it all in," said John Saville, with a smile which robbed his words of all possibility of giving offence. "Nevertheless, I would give much to be able to see the same place, and witness the actual scenes in which a great genius conceived the wonderful inventions which revolutionised the commerce and social relations of the world."

"But you would not appear to venerate Stephenson's inventions very much, since you have discarded them altogether in favour of other systems of locomotion."

"True. But our electric-hydraulic-ways are in reality gradual evolvements arising from the basis afforded by a knowledge of locomotive travelling, as it still existed a few centuries ago. And we can never forget that for some hundreds of years railways were the chief factors of civilisation."

"There is another thing which New Amazonians have discarded, for no sufficient reason it seems to me."

"And that is?"

"Christianity."

"There you labour under a mistake. New Amazonians did not discard Christianity. It was Christianity which declined to help them. When New Amazonia was first peopled by the colonists from Teuto-Scotland, the adult colonists were, as you doubtless know, all women. It was the intention of these women to govern their State with as much success as was compatible with the rejection of conventionality and traditionary laws. It had hitherto been their lot to be excluded from a great proportion of national privileges, which had been usurped by the masculine sex for ages. In casting about for the principal causes of their limitations of fairplay, they found, them, or thought they did so, in the doctrines of Christianity. One of the principal Christian writers indeed, seemed to be quite as much bent upon insulting, humiliating, and subjugating woman, as he was upon spreading the Christian cause. New Amazonian leaders found that they could not take an active part in public affairs without violating all the rules laid down for woman's guidance and man's encouragement by the Apostle Paul. It was a case either of Christianity and reversion to Slavery, or a sort of Unitarianism and Freedom, and they did not hesitate long as to what choice to make. They were not likely, being intelligent beings, to inaugurate a retrogressive movement by instructing their boys in tenets which constantly preached the inferiority and subservence of women, especially as they believed St. Paul's utterances on matters feminine to be dictated more by spite than by honest conviction."

"And what were their grounds for this belief?"

"Their reasons are easily explained. We have it on reliable authority that Saul of Tarsus, whose parents were Greeks, not Jews, but who had himself adopted the Jewish persuasion, was a man of very violent passions and prejudices. He hated the Christians, and took delight in helping to exterminate them. It was when in Jerusalem, bent upon some such mission, that he was introduced to the daughter of the Jewish High Priest, and fell passionately in love with her. To his intense mortification, his proposal for her hand was rejected, and he henceforth hated both women and Jews, becoming enthusiastically Christian by way of a change."

"But, even if this be true, the fact that Paul is not believed in here would hardly account for the repudiation of the doctrines taught by the other apostles of Christianity."

"I think it would. You see, Paul was a man of great ability, who had had the advantage of studying under one of the greatest teachers of the age. His words carried weight with them, and influenced those with whom he associated. His writings and influence are inseparable from Christianity. Even were this not so, there is only too much proof given in History that of all bigots and fanatics, Christian bigots and fanatics are the most cruel, relentless, and implacable. Christ Himself would have repudiated a religion which has made His name an excuse for robbery, oppression, murder, and immorality."

"You surely exaggerate enormously. All Christians disseminate the doctrines preached by Christ in His famous Sermon on the Mount. The Ten Commandments especially are taught to all young Christians."

"Yes, and a fine mockery it has been, to be sure! You will remember that one commandment adjures us to refrain from making 'any graven image, nor the likeness of anything that is in the heaven above, or in the earth beneath, or in the water under the earth.' We are forbidden to bow down to such things, or to worship them. And yet how small a proportion of Christian peoples ever obeyed these injunctions! Until the time of one Martin Luther, God himself was utterly set aside in the Christian churches, which were filled with images and shrines, before which deluded suppliants poured out their vain supplications. Christianity had been entirely supplanted by Idolatry, and existed as such only in name. Again, we are forbidden to take the name of the great Life-giver in vain, and yet what do we find recorded? Priests, calling themselves Christians, professed to have the power to grant forgiveness of sins in the name of the Almighty! Some of these sins were actually *in futuro*, and whether past, or still to be committed, their confession to a priest, accompanied by the gift of a sum of money, ensured a free pardon from Heaven. Of course, the *money* was always required, and those who were too poor to pander to priestly greed were remorselessly consigned to Purgatory. Murder, of course, was strictly forbidden, and yet the advocates of Christianity murdered and tortured thousands of people, simply because they presumed to differ slightly in opinion from those in office. Stealing was prohibited; but the priests were willing to take the last mite from the oppressed poor, rather than abate one jot of their lazy, sensuous privileges. As for the sin of covetousness, in whom has it ever shown itself more rampant than in the men whose chief energies were directed towards appropriating the wealth of all with whom they came in contact, for the joint benefit of themselves and the Church?"

"I grant you all this. But it refers to a state of things which has long since passed away."

"Has image-worship passed away? Do priests work for the pure love of God, or do they look upon their vocation as a means of making a livelihood more to their taste than someothers? Is the priestly office the guerdon of merit and ability? Or is it still the perquisite of those who have money and family influence at command? Do priests exercise universal charity and kindly feeling? Have they given up thinking that none but themselves and a few like-minded individuals will be allowed to enter Heaven? Do they feel as much reverence for goodness in the lowly, as they do for grandeur in high places? Do they discourage the presence in their churches of disreputable persons, if these persons happen to be rich, and are able to be used as pecuniary aids? In a word, are the churches possessed of truly Christ-like qualities, without which none can be a Christian?"

John Saville had by this time worked himself into a perfect glow of enthusiasm, while I certainly felt correspondingly humiliated, for I was not in a position to return an affirmative answer to all his questions.

Did I not remember seeing a man who had not thrown off the effects of the previous night's intoxication officiating in a prominent position, with the priest's approval, in one of our Established churches? Have I not witnessed many another instance of priestly tolerance of evil for Mammon's sake? Have I not recently met with a specimen of clerical intolerance which would do credit to the religious persecutors of old? Candidates for confirmation are requested to confess their crimes to themselves, and to turn from the error of their ways, before they can consider themselves fit to take their stand as Christians. The sins and crimes are presented to the eyes of the penitents in the form of printed questions, and one of these questions runs thus: "Have you ever entered a *Dissenting Chapel*?"

I saw this myself in the year 1889, and was compelled now to admit the conviction that to discard Christ and to discard Christianity may be two very different things. It seemed marvellous, when I came to think of it, how a thinking people like the New Amazonians should, after all these ages, have singled out Christ as the one pure and shining light of earth, so godlike as to be worthy of being at once translated to companionship with the Giver of Life, seeing that His professed devotees have, since the earliest times of the Church, done more to bring His cause into disrepute than all His enemies.

"You admit yourself worsted?" smiled Mr. Saville.

"I confess as much," I replied. "But how comes it that you, a man, should so enthusiastically uphold the only Constitution in the world which has, so far as I know, successfully resisted man's striving for supremacy?"

"Because I am thoroughly satisfied and contented with my lot, and because no country upon earth presents such advantages to her citizens as New Amazonia does. Our women have proved their capacity to govern wisely and well. Our Constitution has found imitators, proof positive that others regard our system with approval. Yet nowhere do we meet with such health and prosperity as in our country, for man's political influence has in all ages proved corruptive and retrogressive. Our health is perfect, and we know that it is to the beneficent rule of our women that we owe our strength of mind and body. It would be suicidal on our part to wish to revert to a state of things which insured us nothing so much as sickly bodies. For how could we expect to be strong and healthy as we are if our mothers were reduced to the condition of the women some of us see when we travel?"

"But do you not find your social masculine disabilities somewhat irritating?"

"We do not labour under any disabilities of importance that I know of. We are not eligible for Political Office, but many men hold important and lucrative posts under Government, in which our administrative talents are given fairplay and in all other respects the educational, social, and elective privileges of the sexes are perfectly equal."

"I am glad to hear such opinions from you. If you could hear the croaking that goes on in my country at the mere prospect of women being allowed to vote, you would wonder at the amount of prejudice and opposition which your ancestresses overcame."

"Well, when you get back to your country, you must try to enlighten your own compatriots."

"Suppose I were never to find my way back, how do you suppose I should fare here? Will the Mother soon be tired of entertaining me?"

"Not just yet, I think. But if your stay with us should prove likely to be permanent, you would yourself most probably desire to make some arrangement whereby you could secure a provision for old age. You probably have been trained to a profession of some kind?"

"No, I have not. I was brought up as the majority of young women in my country are brought up. It was supposed, I expect, that I should settle down in due course, that is, marry, and that an independent profession for myself would not be needed."

"And you say that such folly is the common practice in your country? That accounts for many of the deplorable things you have told me. How can women be independent and free, if they have to rely upon others to keep them? Where is the woman in New Amazonia, do you think, who would care thus to sacrifice her position of self-reliant independence? Such a being does not exist, and I think that your women have themselves or their guardians to thank in great measure for all the disadvantages under which they labour. It will be rather awkward for you, though, if you cannot turn your hand to anything."

"I suppose it would be awkward, if this were so. As it happens, however, I never gave myself up to an idle life, but gradually drifted into literature, and I could probably find employment on one of your numerous journals."

"Certainly. If you are a graphic writer, you are sure of an appointment. Such writers are always welcome, and you must have so much to say. You will not need to cast about long for employment, should it be your

ELIZABETH BURGOYNE CORBETT

lot to remain with us, and you will be able to earn as much as will make ample provision for old age when it comes.

"As you are perhaps aware, a small percentage of our earnings is always appropriated by the State, and a proportionate pension becomes our due as soon as we wish to claim it. If we claim our pension at the age of seventy or eighty, it is relatively smaller than if we wait until our hundredth year or thereabouts. We are usually not in a hurry to place ourselves upon the pension list, for our active period of labour ceases then, and this source of income is lost. Still, if we have filled responsible positions in life, and have been fortunate enough to accumulate wealth, we can, if we like, hand it all over to the State, in return for an augmented annuity. My own parents have done this, and are very happy and comfortable, with not a care in the world.

"There is also another source of profit which we enjoy. New Amazonia is one huge co-operative establishment, for we are all interested in promoting its stability and prosperity. There is another condition, besides being compelled to have reached a certain age, before we can vote at elections. We must all, women and men, purchase a share in the country, and we are all very anxious to do so, seeing that these shares are always at a premium, and command greater returns than any other form of investment."

"Surely this is a source of danger to the community. Could not some people, by purchasing a large number of shares, thus obtain the means of usurping undue power and influence?"

"Impossible! We are not permitted to hold more than one share individually. The idea is to make us all of equal station in the eyes of the law, and to ensure our individual interest in the maintenance of peace and order. When a State bondholder dies, the equivalent of her or his bond is divided amongst such legatees as may have been named in the will."

"And if there is no will?"

"That never happens, for it is compulsory to make a will immediately upon becoming a State shareholder. Of course, if we wish the value of our Bond to revert to the State, we name the State as our legatee, and we are at liberty to alter our will whenever we please."

"You seem to have no money here, other than the all-pervading silver unit. Is this your standard of value in all monetary transactions?"

"Yes; the unit pervades every business transaction, if not practically, at least theoretically. But it is seldom used to pay large amounts with; a paper currency serving our purposes much better than metal coinage would do."

"Are private banks for business houses allowed to issue paper money?"

"No, none but State coupons are permitted to be issued."

"Now, just one more question, and then I have finished. I am told that the State is the ultimate receiver of all manufactured goods, which may neither be retailed nor exported without first yielding the imposed percentage. Is it not possible for a group of speculators to force prices up, either by buying a vast quantity of goods from the manufacturers, and selling at their own price to the State; or, more probable, could they not buy in large quantities from the State, and retail at their own prices to the public?"

"Certainly not. The State would not deal with them. Nor would it permit any increase of prices not necessitated by the legitimate exigencies of trade. Speculators of the class to which you allude would find a sorry field for their operations here."

I could not complain of the amount of information I had obtained from John Saville; but I should probably have been still further enlightened had not our hostess come to claim our attention in different directions. But before saying farewell for the night, he asked me to visit his parents on the day following, and promised me a little enlightenment concerning some domestic arrangements in which I was interested.

ELIZABETH BURGOYNE CORBETT

XV

O n being introduced to John Saville's home, I found a great deal more of simple solid comfort than I had expected, and such an air of domesticity as my own residence in the college had led me to suppose altogether absent from New Amazonian dwellings. At my own request, my visit was of the most informal kind, and not another stranger was there here to disturb the cosiness of the quiet chat which I wished to enjoy.

Mrs. Saville was possessed of the bright brown hair, clear rosy skin, and deep grey eyes, so indicative of pure Irish descent, coupled with a grace and charm of manner I had never seen equalled by an Englishwoman of similar age. Mr. Saville also struck me as just a likely sort of man to be the father of such a clever, popular son. It was clear that they both doted upon him, and just as clear that he would have been sorry to do anything likely to cause them grief.

But they did not treat me to a long category of each other's virtues, preferring to let me form my own opinion of them as individuals, while they did their best to initiate me into the ways of New Amazonian domestic life. Their house consisted of a suite of rooms in a large block of buildings in one of the best parts of Andersonia, and was fitted with even convenience which would conduce to ease and comfort.

The furniture was ideally suitable, good, and elegant, but the pictures on the walls, like many others which I had seen lately, amused me not a little. It seemed to me at first that they were all out of perspective, and that neither walking biped, running quadruped, nor flying bird was painted aright. By-and-bye, however, I got more used to these pictorial oddities, and caught myself thinking that when I got home again, I should be wanting to introduce some of these Muybridgeian notions into my own rooms.

The fire cast a comfortable glow on all around, making it difficult to believe that the problem of fuel for the future was now definitely settled, and that electricity could now and henceforth be made to supply the necessary fuel for warming, lighting, cooking, and manufacturing purposes. No dirt or dust from ashes, and no discoloration as the result of burning gas was here felt, for neither the one nor the other were now in use. Both had served humanity well in their day. Both were now superseded by a much more efficient, cleanly, and convenient agent.

After our very appetising evening meal had been despatched; I was taken on a tour of inspection round the building, or, rather, round such parts of it as were public to all the tenants. The basement consisted entirely of shops, which were connected by means of telephones with every suite in the block, and could, with the aid of electric lifts, supply anything ordered per telephone at a moment's notice. Nor was there any fear of extortionate charges, or a poor sample of goods, since everything had to be priced according to the day's Government scale, and the daily visits of Government inspectors ensured the withdrawal of inferior or unwholesome articles.

While conversing on telephonic subjects, I mentioned that even in my benighted country we had made good use of this valuable invention. "There are even telephones attached to churches and theatres," I said, "by means of which a sermon or a song may be heard at great distances from the places in which they are delivered. But of course you have even improved upon these notions?"

"I think we have," smiled Mrs. Saville. "Some hundreds of years ago there was hardly a building in New Amazonia which was not a perfect network of telephones and patent lifts, and our people began to give the Mother considerable anxiety, for they showed rapid signs of deterioration. On looking round for the causes of this unfortunate falling back, it was found to be produced by the mania for saving labour and exercise of every possible sort, and drastic measures were speedily introduced.

"Many of the lifts were abolished, and substantial staircases erected in their stead, up and down which the people were expected to walk when going in or out. The goods lifts were, however, not considered too provocative of laziness and inactivity, and still remain very useful adjuncts to civilization.

"The telephone system, though disapproved of by the Mother, did not require quite such stringent measures to make it almost a thing of the past, so far as mere amusement is concerned.

"When it first became possible to hear a concert or lecture without being compelled to leave one's own house, everybody went in for this sort of spiritless amusement. But it soon palled upon the people, for there is no comparison between such a namby-pamby apology for social enjoyment, and the pleasure to be derived from sitting within sight of the speakers or musicians, and taking in their general appearance, gestures, and accessories. Curiosity will always be one of the strongest elements in human composition, and no social pleasure is perfect which does not permit the eyes to aid the ears in their appreciation of the fare offered to them. When, therefore, the novelty of telephonic entertainments was over, the people tired of them, and hardly cared to listen to the amusing or instructive sounds they had paid their money to ensure. And when, a few years later, the Government imposed a tax upon the use of all telephones not of a strictly useful or business nature, the *coup de grâce* was given to the stay-at-home-and-enjoy-the-concert-at-your-ease system, and we have never reverted to it since."

After that, I thought, I will be careful about boasting of English progress, since what we deem the summit of luxurious ease is here looked upon as the babyhood of true civilization.

"And did the reforms you mention produce the results which Government aimed at?" I enquired aloud.

"Yes," was the reply. "Bodily health and strength depend in great measure upon a rational exercise of our physical capabilities. The more exercise of a reasonable nature we take, the stronger and the more capable of work and enjoyment are we. The more we give way to indolence, and yield to the temptation to stay indoors, the more demoralized and unfit for the daily duties of life do we become. To encourage anything that produces physical deterioration is to retard our chances of attaining spiritual perfection, and is too dear a price to pay for such unsatisfactory results."

While talking, we were making due progress in our investigations, and by this time had come to a part of the building which filled me with admiring wonder. A large brass plate affixed to a massive door informed me that these were the premises of the Domestic Aid Society. On touching an electric bell, the door opened, and showed us a spacious vestibule, at one side of which was situated the office of the check-clerk, whose vocation it was to keep a strict account of all comings and goings, and register the orders and commissions which were constantly coming in per telephone from different parts of this and other buildings in the city.

This, it seemed, was visitors' day, and we proceeded to inspect the Domestic Aid Society's premises at our leisure. The first room we entered was a working hall, in which members of both sexes were busily engaged in fashioning various articles for personal and household use. It was a species of dressmaking, millinery, tailoring, and plain sewing establishment all rolled into one.

The room was comfortably and artistically furnished. The presses for storing materials and work were elaborately carved, and pleasant to look upon. The light, warmth, and ventilation were all perfect, and I could not help thinking how delighted a London worker would be, if privileged to labour in such pleasant quarters. No wonder everybody looked happy and healthy here, since even the most humble in the land were ensured perfect sanitary surroundings, and limited hours of work.

Another room that pleased me exceedingly was the cookery. Here, for the benefit of those who preferred to order their supplies ready for the table, every branch of the culinary art was in progress, from the making of plain bread to the concoction of the most delicate dainties. The walls of the cookery were covered with white tiles; the floor was white, the tables were immaculate, and the cooks and confectioners were spotlessly neat and clean.

There was neither fuss, heat, nor discomfort, as is the case in England when a great deal of cooking has to be done, for the work was done systematically, and the greatest pains had been taken to make all the conditions of labour as pleasant as possible.

Our next visit was made to the laundry, and it was a treat to see how science had been brought to bear upon the solution of the greatest problem which my own countrywomen are beset with, viz., how to minimise the labour and discomfort which with us so invariably attend washing days. From beginning to end, nearly every laundry operation was conducted by means of noiseless electric machinery, manipulated by skilled workpeople who knew their work to be quite as valuable, and much more necessary, than the productions of those who followed the purely ornamental arts.

In response to my questions on the subject, Mrs. Saville gave me the following information:—

"The Domestic Aid Society is one of the most popular of all New Amazonian institutions, and there are establishments of this sort all over the country. They are generally the property of private individuals, but are strictly subjected to State supervision and regulation. The books are kept with the utmost exactness, and there is never any difficulty in apportioning the share of profit which is due to the Mother. The workpeople, no matter in what department they may be, are all, with the exception of the supervisors and learners, paid on the same scale. This enables our people to make their choice of a vocation in favour of the employment they fancy most, without financial or social reasons requiring to be taken into consideration, since both pay and position are equal. The hours are from seven in the morning until five at night, with intervals for meals. All work out of these hours is paid for on a special scale. Besides the specialists whom you have seen, there are many people employed by the Domestic Aid Societies. We charter for servants by the day, week, or month, who come at the time agreed upon and discharge any household duties which we may wish to entrust to them. Messengers are also supplied for a trifling commission. Our domestic work is always well done, for the assistants are trained by the State, and are interested in securing our goodwill, as a bonus is attached to the successful completion of a lengthened term of service in one household. It is not often that we wish our assistants to be changed, for the very fact of knowing that we have only to telephone to the office to effect any change we desire, does away with the irascibility so often engendered by the ancient system of engaging servants for long periods, and being compelled to find sleeping accommodation for them. We are not, however, in any case, addicted to finding unnecessary faults in our assistants, for all our complaints are registered, and if it is found that we are exceptionally bad to please, we have to pay a slightly augmented tariff by way of atoning for our unpleasant peculiarities."

"And how do these domestic helps employ their time when not on active duty? And what is their relative position as compared with skilled workpeople? Is their work regarded as inferior?"

"By no means. Domestic assistants occupy a very honourable position in our social economy, for they, like others, have to go through a careful course of training, and fulfil very important duties. Their scale of pay is good, and it is by no means difficult for them to purchase a State-Coupon, if they are thrifty. Their spare time is employed in consonance with their own inclinations. There is a fine recreation hall attached to every Domestic Agency in the country. In these our working classes can enjoy themselves to their heart's content, by means of social converse, music, reading, dancing, or games of skill."

"This question of working classes *versus* educated classes is a very potent one with us. Class prejudice is strong, and our aristocracy would not submit to associate with artisans or domestic assistants on such equal terms as is habitual with you, unless, indeed, one of them were to succeed to a fortune, and then all her or his vulgarities and shortcoming would find plenty of consideration. How do you account for the superior element of sociality in your country?"

"Easily. We are all educated on the same footing. Some of us develop literary, artistic, or scientific instincts early in life, and speedily find our vocation. Others whose full brain powers are not yet developed, or who are diffident of their own ability to adopt one of the higher professions, choose a mechanical training, and discover afterwards that they have missed their *forte*. Nothing daunted, they employ their leisure in retrieving lost ground, and while possibly serving in the capacity of domestic help, may be qualifying for classical or surgical examinations, and may even at some distant date be privileged to become Leaders. We respect mental and moral greatness, even if in embryo, and never object to society that is pleasant in itself."

"What a paradisaical state of things," I sighed, fervently. "You can do nothing in my country without plenty of money, and, for the matter of that, how do your erstwhile inferiorities succeed in reaching positions of eminence, seeing that they must have heavy examination fees to pay, for which the adequate amount can hardly be saved out of working class wages? Or does the State provide examiners free of charge?"

"No. Our examiners, as you may easily suppose, are very responsible, and, therefore, very well-paid officials. But they are not a source of expense to the Government, because the scale of examination fees is such as to leave a substantial margin of State profit. Want of funds is never an obstacle to progress here, for candidates for examination are permitted to pay the fees from their future earnings."

"And suppose they were inclined to forget the repayment part of the business, what then?"

At this question, my hearers looked so astounded that I felt painfully conscious of having committed a huge blunder, the nature of which was soon made evident to me by the reply I received. "You must really come from a very strange country," said John Saville, fortunately for my composure, in the pleasantest of tones, "for such a question to be possible to you. The individual who could thus think of cheating would not be a New Amazonian. But, even if this were so, the Mother has the remedy in her own hands. She would withhold the pension to which we are all honourably entitled in old age."

"As you imply," I responded deprecatively, "my people are not like your people, so you must excuse the ignorance which prompted what is evidently an offensive question. I wish I could say as much for English national morality as you can for yours. But it is a painful fact that fully one-half of the English race subsists upon the results of the crimes or follies of the other half. I prefer, however, to talk of local topics, and learn all I can of your social system while I have the opportunity. You

ELIZABETH BURGOYNE CORBETT

will, therefore, I hope, not consider me very troublesome, if I ask yet another question or two."

"We shall be only too happy to afford you any assistance in our power," replied Mr. Saville.

"Then," I said, "can you tell me how a large business, say, a Domestic Aid Agency, would fare, if the business done were inadequate, or the capital subscribed too small? Would the proprietors become bankrupt, or would the Mother help them out of their difficulties?"

"Bankruptcy is, I believe, an obsolete term, implying that the subject of it has contracted debts which she or he does not intend to pay. Such things do not occur here. If we order a thing, and reap the benefit of it, nothing but death itself exonerates us from ultimate payment. If a business is not prospering, application is usually made to the proper authorities to institute an investigation and assist us out of our difficulties. Should it prove that our incapacity is at the root of the evil, we are advised to adopt some less onerous mode of earning a livelihood, and our proportion of the liabilities is discharged by the State, and accredited to us for future repayment. If, however, mere lack of capital is cramping our operations, the State supplies the necessary impetus, and constitutes itself an active partner, by purchasing as many shares as will float the business financially, and by appointing a Government agent to assist in the management. In fact, there is not a business of any magnitude in the land in which the Mother is not a partner, and, in addition, she of course takes the percentage of the profits, which in other countries is raised unjustly and unequally by means of clumsily imposed taxes."

"As with us, in fact."

"Is this so? I must know a little more of this very-much-behind-the-times country of yours, which you call England. England, as known to us, ceased to exist centuries ago, and yet you have spoken of living in the vicinity of the home of George Stephenson. How this can be, I cannot understand. We know that when he lived, the neighbouring island, now called Teuto-Scotland, was called England. But we also know that hundreds of years are supposed to have passed since the last vestige of Stephenson's Northumbrian home was destroyed. How do you explain such anomalies?"

So spoke Mr. Saville, and the rest of our conversation consisted of explanations and descriptions on my own part which proved intensely interesting to the Saville family, but which would sound so much like an oft-told tale to my readers, that I refrain from inflicting it upon them.

XVI

After all this conversation we were in the mood to enjoy the dainty meal spread before us. The young woman in attendance was one of the employés of the Domestic Agency, and had served Mrs. Saville, to their mutual satisfaction, for five years. She moved about the room with a grace born of her perfect physical training, which I would fain see prevalent in my own country. In response to a question of John Saville's, she informed us that there was to be a grand amateur theatrical entertainment in the Recreation Hall that evening, at which she intended to be one of the performers.

As she was one of the indoor servants of the Agency, and slept in the building, she was practically at home during most of her hours of recreation, and she spoke with all the verve and vigour of one who enjoyed life to the utmost. She was merry without familiarity; energetic without being fussy; and respectful without being servile—altogether the very *beau idéal* of a nice-looking and intelligent waiting maid.

As I noted herself and her ways critically, I thought that there was really no reason why we should not establish these Domestic Aid Agencies in England. We are not usually very slow in adopting socially economic ideas which have once suggested themselves to us, and if enterprise and capital united were to take the notion up, the chief sources of English domestic worry would be soon put an end to, as would also the reluctance of respectable girls to adopt what is at present in only too many cases nothing better than a life of dull, miserable slavery.

The meal ended, and the things all cleared away, Alice O'Reilly's work for the day was over, and she betook herself to her own quarters, in order to prepare for the evening's innocent jollities, while we again reverted to our comparisons of the social conditions of our respective countries. I believe that the hardest nut which I gave the Saville family to crack was my statement that when I last remembered being at home, the English Government had consigned some zealous partisans of Irish liberty to the temporary seclusion of some gaols in Ireland, which I was now assured had long ceased to exist. It was in vain that I insisted; and when I spoke of Queen Victoria, Mr. Gladstone, and Mr. Parnell as living contemporaneously with myself, the amusement of my friends was, in its turn, amusing to witness.

"I wouldn't be surprised, after that," said John Saville, "to hear that you claim personal acquaintance with the immortal writer of Hamlet and Macbeth."

"Do you allude to Shakespeare or Bacon?" I queried innocently.

"Bacon? I know nothing of Bacon," retorted John Saville. "But I am very much in love with the works of a certain William Shakespeare."

"You think you are. Shakespeare did not write the plays bearing his name. The real author was Bacon, as several individuals have set themselves to prove."

"I am afraid they have proved their case but badly. For while all our scholars have Shakesperian quotations at their tongues' ends, there is not one of us who has ever heard a whisper of any presumed Baconian origin of our best loved classics."

Poor Mr. Donnelly!

From playwright to novelist was a natural transition; and, remembering sundry financial bruisings in connection with the publication of one of my earliest and lengthiest novels, a glow of exultation possessed me when I learnt the conditions under which books were published nowadays.

The long-suffering author had triumphed at last, and his erstwhile oppressor was shorn of his glory. I was told that the State had established an immense Literary Bureau, with which large printing and publishing works were associated. All works other than already licensed newspapers and magazines intended for publication were submitted in the first instance to the Bureau, and read by the official censor.

If found to be innocent of offences against morality, the book was taken in hand, and published under State authority, the author paying the whole of the cost, and receiving the whole of the future emoluments, subject to the five percent tax accruing to the State. There was no arbitrary range of charges, but a scale of payment for work done which was sufficient to repay the State outlay, *plus* a slight percentage of profit. Writers could, by studying the printed tariff, know exactly what style and quality of material and workmanship to choose, and would also know to a fraction what their expenses would be. Nor did present lack of funds stand in the way of success, for the State helped capable, industrious authors by a judicious system of credit, just as it helped any other of its people who had done nothing to forfeit the supposition that they were deserving of such assistance. As already pointed out, State aid within certain limits was unattended with any risk to the Government, as it had means of repaying itself.

The law of copyright was simplicity itself. For one hundred years the copyright was the inalienable property of the author, or the author's nominees. At the end of that time the State succeeded to all copyrights as were still of value. No grasping publisher was allowed to step in and reap the profits of an author's brain toil, and there was no gall mixed with the thought that a work was being written which might possibly survive to become a valuable property of the nation, even as Gibbons' "Decline and Fall of the Roman Empire" is still a gold mine to enterprising and speculative publishers in England.

There was no sort of hesitation on the part of anyone to claim of the "Mother" the help and protection to which, as her veritable children, they were justly entitled. Pauperism and workhouses did not exist, simply because the State saw the wisdom of preventing squalor and destitution by its system of claiming the care of its people from their infancy, and being generous in its mode of launching them in life.

When we reflect upon the enormous sums which are collected for poor rates in England, it is easy to conceive the vast social improvement the same amount of money and labour could produce, if spent in the education and fair start in life of our thousands of miserable and squalid gutter-birds, who, instead of being all their life-long a continual source of expense to the nation, would grow up respectable and respected units of society, abhorring the life of shame and degradation which they and only too many others look upon at present as their natural birthright.

"Prevention is better than cure," is just as trite and useful a maxim for the State as it is for the subject, as is also the warning against being "penny-wise and pound-foolish." It would cost much less for our country to feed, clothe, educate, and train to useful avocations half-a-million youngsters taken from the slums, than it would cost to meet one-half of the expenses that same half-million of juveniles will provide for their compatriots before they have run the course of drunkenness, pauperism, misery, and crime which the laws of cause and effect have only too surely marked out for them in the unhappy future.

When comparing New Amazonia with England, another idea suggests itself. How much of the national prosperity I saw around me was owing to the fact that New Amazonia was free from the incubus of having to provide vast sums for the support of a monarchy which with us is exceedingly limited in its beneficent effects, but which possesses an unlimited capacity for appropriating huge emoluments which would be more sensibly spent in liquidating the National Debt, or in alleviating some of the national misery! If saddled with the incalculable burdens which England has to bear, even New Amazonian rulers would find it a difficult task to present a satisfactory budget at the end of their term of office.

There is also another way in which our poor are deprived of a great deal of help they would otherwise receive. Many of our churches and chapels are simply begging houses, in which their frequenters are persuaded to part with every penny they can be induced to spare. And this, if the donors are satisfied, is perfectly right in its way. But is it right that while countless poor souls, old and young, are rotting, body and soul, in our own land, it should be the boast of our Missionary Societies that they give hundreds of thousands of pounds every year to strangers who do not need the gospel preached practically to them half so much as the miserable denizens of the back slums of our own parishes?

The zeal of the advocates of Foreign missions is commendable, but I respectfully submit that it is misdirected, and if some of them had half an idea of what only too often ultimately becomes of their money, they would be very chary about subscribing in future.

But when even those whose office and mission it is to seek and succour their poor and needy neighbours, find their time and attention taken up with more distant and less pressing duties, how is it likely that our legislators, occupied so intensely as they are in trying to prove each other unfit for office, will ever find time to take the cause of the social improvement of the people into consideration? It is hopeless to think of it at present, for a true and tender interest will never be felt in the units of the nation until our Constitution becomes less that of rulers and ruled, and more like that of mother and children.

To this devoutly-to-be-hoped-for consummation there is another obstacle. The truly maternal instinct has no equivalent in the breast of man, and so long as none but men are the people's representatives, even so long will that people be deprived of a thousand rights which a just, earnest, womanly co-government would give them. It is monstrous to speak of women as being even incapable of voting wisely, when they have already proved themselves capable of governing much more judiciously than men, many of whom seem to recognise no other legitimate result of taking office than squabbling and banqueting.

Certainly in many cases these are about the only matters to which some of our corporate bodies devote their attention, and surely, surely feminine nincompoopery could go no further than this!

There is a town in Kansas, called Oskaloosa, of which the Mayor and other members of the Corporation are all women. Their first term of office has been so triumphantly progressive that they have been enthusiastically re-elected, and within twelve months the place has made such wonderful strides in the trifling matters of social morality, sanitation, and prosperity, that it is the wonder of surrounding towns.

After so signal a proof of feminine capacity, it argues great paucity of brains for anyone to insinuate that a clever, capable woman is less able to form a sensible opinion as to the relative merits of candidates for office than a man who perhaps spends half his days in loafing about public houses or race courses, and half his nights in dens of infamy. A truly moral judgment we need expect from such truly moral voters!

I meet an individual in the street. His legitimate avocation is that of bird-catching. He has been doing good business, and has spent part of his precarious earnings in sundry "two-pennorths" of gin, and in a paper of vile tobacco. He positively reeks of low life, and pollutes the atmosphere as he staggers through the streets. An unfortunate dog crosses his path. He gives it a vicious kick, and sends it howling and limping to a neighbouring cabmen's shelter for sympathy. The dog's howls remind him of the miserable wife and children at home who are destined to feel the weight of his kicks and blows, and a demoniac, exulting grin of conscious masculine superiority spreads over his face, while he unconsciously increases his speed, in order the sooner to be at the game he loves above all others.

Am I to believe that this thing is better able to judge of the merits of a candidate for electoral honours than I am simply because it is a Man?

Am I to assume that this reptile is legally and morally better fitted to take a place among our legislators than I, solely because it is a Man?

Perish the thought! Man's arrogance and woman's cowardice have reigned long enough, and it behoves my countrywomen to assert their rights and privileges without further delay.

Never mind what the men say. They cannot say more than they have said. Never mind what the *weak-minded* women say. Their opinions are not worth heeding.

We are beginning to understand all we have been deprived of. We have clear ideas as to what we want. We are perfectly aware that we have an uphill fight, and plenty of senseless opposition to encounter. But we also know that "Patience overcometh all things."

Woman has up to now proved that she is superabundantly gifted

ELIZABETH BURGOYNE CORBETT

with a spurious, undesirable sort of patience. It has hitherto been of the passive and take-things-as-a-matter-of-course kind. All that wants altering. Patience still, if you like. But it must be active, and coupled with such steady determination as shall ensure the realisation of all our hopes, and make political and social equality of the sexes a realisation of the near future.

And, now, I am struck with another idea. It has suddenly occurred to me that I have wandered a long way from the Savilles, and that my readers will wonder where I intend to pick them up again. I have really, however, not very far to go, for they are originally responsible for all the digression which their conversation has suggested, and if the opinions feebly expressed in the preceding pages succeed in winning a few recruits to the cause of progress, the Saville family would not be disposed to cavil at my momentary neglect of them.

I recall a remark John Saville made during that memorable visit.

"Suppose," he said, "I were to find this fabulous country of yours, and were to set up as a lecturer, how do you think I should succeed?"

"That depends upon the subjects chosen. I do not doubt your power to express your views forcibly."

"Well, I will give you a short syllabus. I would extol our methods of dealing with children, in preference to yours. I would impress upon all young women the folly of permitting my sex to arrogate to itself the right to be the first to speak of matters amorous or matrimonial. I would scout the idea of women being paid less wages than men, when the work done by both is identically the same in quality and quantity. I would insist not merely upon woman's electoral rights, but upon woman's equal right with man to govern her country. You see, I am not quite going the length of leaving us poor men out in the cold altogether. How do you think my programme will take?"

"Indifferently well."

"Why?"

"Because you would be lecturing in opposition to the 'no progress' views of the majority of your hearers."

"But I have understood you to say that your country boasts far more women than men. How then could I, the 'Woman's Apostle,' be in the minority?"

"Because you would not merely have the opposition of men to overcome, but would have arrayed against you the prejudices of all those women who are too bigoted in their own ignorance to know what is good for themselves or others, and their name is legion. You see, the process of education in the doctrines of the necessity for self-assertion and personal effort is still young, and until we can awaken the self-respect, which it has been for ages the mission of men to extinguish in women, we cannot hope to effect the results which demand united action. Still, the 'Onward' portion of my sex grows in numbers every year, as does also the number of our masculine supporters, and I hope to win an immense number of recruits when I get home again, and describe all I have seen here."

"And that reminds me. How do you propose to get home?"

"Well, really, I—. Upon my word, I don't know. I suppose, however, that I shall be able to discover some way of reaching England, when I have solved the preliminary problem of earning the necessary funds. I have already written some descriptive articles, which I hope will be accepted."

"They are sure to be accepted, and well paid for into the bargain, for everything connected with you has roused the greatest interest in the country. So the question of your independence is settled already. But even were this not so, the Mother is always kind, and would provide you with the means of travelling. The difficulty lies in discovering your actual destination."

"If this is really Ireland in a perfected state, I have not far to go. A country may be revolutionised and improved by social reforms, but nothing of much less power than an earthquake can remove it altogether. If England stands where it did, I have but to take a boat to Holyhead, and a few hours more will take me home to Northumberland."

"And what will you do when you get there?"

"Report myself to my friends without further delay."

"You forget that you must have been sleeping some centuries, and that you are not likely to find any friends left alive, or any place you have known, in the same condition as that in which you left it. Look at this map. Here is the island of which you speak. Holyhead and Northumberland still find their place upon it. But is all else as you left it?"

I eagerly looked at the map before me, and without difficulty pounced upon Newcastle. But where were all the outlying villages which used to assert themselves so independently and with such "plum"-like utterance?

Gone! Everyone of them. Swallowed up in the huge advance of their powerful centre, Newcastle-on-Tyne. I looked for Benwell, Gosforth,

Scotswood, Lemington, Newburn, Benton, Killingworth, and a dozen other places, all in vain, for Newcastle overspread them all, and, as the veritable Metropolis of the North, presented a picture of progress and prosperity which were amazing to me.

I was told that centuries of effort had made the Tyne one of the noblest rivers in the land. Fleets could ride upon its waters in safety, and it was now an important naval station. Its commercial relations with the rest of the world were enormous. In arts and manufactures it was alike distinguished, and it was the most famous place in all Europe for the production of every kind of electrical apparati, besides being the northern centre of learning.

Countless other improvements and aggrandisements were related to me, but for the most part they fell on deaf ears at the time.

I had at last realised that I was bereft of everybody and everything I had ever held dear, and must henceforth consider myself alone in the world, an alien in a strange land, without the possibility of ever again exchanging a word or look of affection with those whom I had loved well and truly.

No wonder my fortitude gave way. No wonder I returned to the college in a mood bordering on despair.

XVII

M y earnest consideration for the next few days was devoted to the question of ways and means. Knowing it to be the custom of the country to entertain strangers hospitably, I had hitherto accepted the attentions offered me in the frank, cordial spirit in which they were given. But this could not continue beyond a reasonable term, and now that my stay in the country seemed likely to be permanent, myself-respect demanded that I should at once take steps to prove my capability of assuming an active part in the battle of life.

As before hinted, I was not likely to encounter many difficulties in the way of earning a livelihood, for my own experiences were a subject of such interest to New Amazonians, that sketches of them would easily find a market in the native journals. In fact, even while debating the point with myself, Principal Grey came to me as the bearer of a message from the Mother.

She was deputed to ask me if I purposed making Andersonia my permanent abiding place, and I was also requested to state my views for the future in any case. She was somewhat surprised to find me full of grief at the conviction that I had indeed parted forever from all and everything which I had ever loved, and she did her utmost to console me, some of her utterances dwelling in my memory yet.

"It has certainly struck us as a great wonder," she said, "that you should have appeared so strangely in our midst. Some of our savants have had discussions on the subject, but can come to no rational solution of the questions mooted. To believe that you were magically transported hither, is revolting to our twenty-fifth century common sense, especially as we can locate no country which is in the condition described by you as that of your native land. To believe that you have been in a state of torpidity for six hundred years seems more likely. But if we accept this hypothesis, we are confronted with the problem of accounting for your whereabouts prior to your resuscitation. There has been found not a single trace of your resting place. Had you been borne hither on the wings of the wind, your advent could not have been more mysterious, nor more bereft of all clue as to your former place of abode. Your own utterances, and those of your odd compatriot, only seem to leave one opinion open to us, and that is, that you have been in a state of trance. The descriptions you have given of your own country and its state of civilisation, as known to you, tally exactly with what is known of Teuto-Scotland as it existed in the nineteenth century. The fact that you call it England puts us, of course, on the right track at once. But whatever may account for your arrival here, it is an undoubted fact that you are of as real flesh and blood as we are, and that you are now leading as commonplace a life as any of us. This being so, it is expedient that some plans should be laid for your future, and I, as the Mother's representative, am deputed to elicit your views and intentions on the subject. That you should only just have realised the impossibility of finding England or its inhabitants as you left them possibly makes my errand appear somewhat in-apropos and precipitate to you. I have, however, my instructions to carry out, and you must forgive me, if it should strike you as rather unfeeling to enquire what you intend to do for a livelihood?"

"I could not possibly take offence where all have shown me so much kindness and consideration," was my reply. "I was, in fact, just deliberating the same subject when you came. I have been encouraged to think that I may hope to get on in the vocation to which I have already devoted some years of apprenticeship—that of an author."

"Yes, that is the opinion we have also formed, and it is in connection therewith that I have a proposal to make to you. Will you write a book descriptive of your former life, associates, and customs? The Literary Bureau will publish it for you, and as there is sure to be a huge demand for it, your profits will be large enough to justify the State in at once presenting you with advance Letters of Credit. These Letters of Credit, as you know, represent money with us, and if you undertake to write this work, considering it a State commission, you will at once find yourself in a position of independence."

What other answer than "Yes" could I give to such a wonderful proposal as this? A certain very nice, but rather gushing, young lady whom I know would have at once exclaimed, "Oh! it's *too* lovely." I did not do that, but I managed to express my thanks and my acquiescence with such a mixture of enthusiasm and dignity as did justice alike to my desire to show my gratitude and to my sense of my own importance.

Let not the reader imagine that I had no legitimate room for the latter feeling, for I was undoubtedly a very prominent and important personage in New Amazonia. Circumstances over which I had had no control had placed me in a position of publicity which was none the less real because it was none of my seeking. The probabilities were in favour of my popularity dying out as soon as I became less of a novelty.

Meanwhile it was advisable that I should take the goods with which the gods had provided me, and make the most of the opportunities thrown in my way.

It did not take long to arrange my subsequent programme. I was to commence writing on the following day, and to submit my work weekly to the Bureau, which would make such arrangements as its heads might think fit for bringing my work under the notice of the public.

Still, in spite of the interesting nature of our conversation, I could not repress my melancholy, and was so depressed that my companion offered the consolatory remark, "That though I was parted from my beloved ones so long as I remained in my own probationary state, they were not deprived of the power of knowing my whereabouts, and were probably rejoicing at the fact that I had been placed in a sphere of action which could not fail to assist my attempts to perfect myself for the higher life."

I was conscious of finding a little consolation in the Principal's arguments, and remarked that it would have been some additional comfort to me if I could have known where my dear ones were buried, so that, though deprived of their society, I might at least do honour to them by visiting and adorning their last resting place.

The Principal did not exactly grasp my meaning at first. When she did, she was horrified.

"Is it possible," she cried in amaze, "that you can contemplate with equanimity the prospect of being laid in the ground to rot in repulsive putrefaction? to be the prey of vermin; to pollute the earth, air, and water around you; and to be the source of death and disease to those whom you have left behind? It is too horrible to think of!"

"Why, what would you have us do?" I enquired blankly. "You wouldn't have us kept above ground, would you?"

"I would have you decently cremated, as we all are when we die. How can you expect to be healthy in mind and body, surrounded by the miasmatic emanations of putrifying corpses? It was demonstrated to New Amazonian satisfaction centuries ago that it would be impossible to rid the land of fever and pestilential diseases until this principal source of water pollution was removed. We still have pictures of ancient graveyards, and I can very well imagine what they were like. The hoary, venerable looking church; the funny upright slabs of stone or marble marking the place where several bodies were undergoing the putrefactive process; the pretty flowers and the picturesque trees; the little brooklet, which winds its rippling way through or past the churchyard; its water, looking pure and limpid because it has percolated its way through the dead and decaying remains of your ancestors, and bearing no easily discernible evidence of the deadly impurities of which it is the conveying medium; I see them all, and can even follow the little brooklet as it feeds the waters of a larger stream, and finally becomes a component part of some great river, from which the water supply of one of your immense manufacturing towns is obtained. Very interesting as a picture, no doubt, but when you quietly contemplate the calm endurance of such a horrible state of things—Faugh!"

Certainly, as presented by the Principal, the picture was not a nice one. But one does not relinquish all one's most sentimental customs without a struggle, and a warm discussion ensued between us, from which, however, I emerged the loser, as I might have expected. When I came to think of it, it was not pleasant to reflect that every drink of water I had ever had had possibly meandered its way through the dissolving tissues of some recently departed victim of cholera or fever. Even the idea of past near relationship to the too generously diffusive corpse was not consolatory, for it had a sort of cannibalistic aspect about it which did not argue true affection for the departed.

I remembered that in my country one of the chief objections to cremation, apart from the purely sentimental reasons promulgated, was that in cases of foul play the process annihilated all chances of ever discovering the real cause of death, as no analysis of cremated remains can be made. On reflection, it struck me that it was less important that one malefactor should be brought to book, than that whole communities should be exposed to the risk of poison.

I reflected also that the system of "Life Insurance" was mainly responsible for the crimes of our modern poisoners. Given the abolition of a system whereby our relatives and guardians are interested in our speedy demise, and the substitution of the plan which prevailed in New Amazonia, whereby every child of the State had its old age provided for, and poisoning, by becoming so evidently useless, would at the same time become our rarest crime.

So I thought, while admitting to Principal Grey that burial was a dangerous and unsatisfactory mode of disposing of the dead.

By-and-bye we began to talk of other things, and in the course of conversation it occurred to me to make some enquiries relating to Mr. Augustus Fitz-Musicus and his future plans.

"I am afraid," was the rejoinder, "that Mr. Fitz-Musicus can never be converted into a sober New Amazonian. He has revolted against wearing our National costume, and says that rather than sacrifice his British individuality, and look like everybody else, he will brave the probability of becoming a laughing-stock, and that he will wear his old clothes to rags rather than have his individuality swallowed up in a general resemblance to every nincompoop in the country. I am afraid it would necessitate him to live as long again as he has done, to bring him into the exact likeness of a native of New Amazonia. But his vanity is inextinguishable, and nothing could bring him to the belief that his appearance does not eclipse that of our handsomest men. When last I heard of him, he was seeking some stuff with a large pattern. He says that if he can find a nice big check, he may perhaps consent to have a suit made in native style, but he is not at all sure yet."

"But how does he intend earning his living?"

"He is not at all sure about that either. He says that he will think about it. But he protests meanwhile very bitterly against a destiny that has placed him among people who can be sordid and vulgar enough to ask him, the pampered scion of a great house, to degrade himself by attempting to earn his own living. He considers that the Mother ought to be proud of being honoured by his sojourn amongst us, and that she ought to be only too glad to extend her hospitality indefinitely to him."

"And the Mother—what does she think of his peculiarities? Are they found annoying?"

"Well, to a certain extent, yes. We abhor ingratitude. But in this case, we are being forced into the belief that this Englishman is not exactly a responsible agent. I am afraid that he is not quite sane. But, of course, unless he becomes very much worse, it will not be found necessary to adopt stringent measures with him."

"And if his peculiarities should become much more pronounced?"

"Ah, then—then, we shall be compelled to do something. He has already lost so much time during his prolonged state of unconsciousness, that it will be a charity to release his spirit, if it becomes evident that it is withheld from further progress towards Heavenly bliss by being confined in a body which is more likely to promote retrogression than progression."

As I listened to this calm utterance my blood positively ran cold. Full well I knew what she meant. The peculiar tenets of New Amazonian religion had been carefully explained to me, and I knew that the life of

Mr. Fitz-Musicus was destined to be a short one, unless he restored the native belief in his sanity. I was quite unable to talk much more after this, and my friend, observing that I seemed fatigued and had better rest, left me to my own resources. But I felt incapable of resting, for I was too excited. Clearly the life of the eccentric Augustus was in danger, and I was impatient to see him and warn him without delay.

I knew where he was located for the present, and I resolved to see him at the earliest opportunity. All night I was restless and perturbed, and though six o'clock was still early for the British masher, I dressed myself with my usual care and set off to visit him, knowing that we should have a better chance of talking undisturbed by taking a morning stroll together, than if I waited until we were both in the midst of society. Besides, I had to begin my book, and I intended working honestly to discharge my debt to New Amazonia.

As I had partly expected, Mr. Fitz-Musicus was not yet astir, and when he ultimately presented himself, he was in a state of supreme conjecture as to my reasons for having him roused so unseasonably.

"Upon my life," he grumbled discontentedly, "one gets no peace in this miserable place. Only yesterday I was asked in cold blood to select some way of earning my own livelihood. Me! who never had even to dress myself without assistance until I came to this benighted land. And, now, you come and rouse me at this unconscionable time. I would like to catch a servant of ours seizing me by the shoulder and making me get up at this time in the morning, like that fellow did just now. I would not only have packed him about his business, but would have refused him a character into the bargain. But in this confounded country there is no freedom. One cannot do as one likes and an impudent boot cleaner actually presumes to dictate to a Fitz-Musicus! And then the women are such fools, too. They cannot appreciate a good chance when they get it. I have proposed to no less than six of them, and what do you think they all did? Nothing but laugh, upon my word! They didn't believe that I really meant to throw myself away upon them, and when I tried to convince them that I was actually in earnest, they just grew more dense and unbelieving, and laughed all the more. An Englishwoman would have sense enough to jump at such an offer, and I don't think I shall demean myself by proposing to another New Amazonian."

"I don't think I would," I rejoined as gravely as I could. "They do not know how to appreciate you. Still, I think that you are not quite fair to the land of your adoption. Personally, I have found nothing to grumble at."

"Oh! with you it is different. You see I have been used to every consideration all my life long, while you have never been anything but a mere nobody."

"Precisely so. But you will forgive me, if I remark that your sense of personal importance is running away with your discretion, and is likely to lead you into trouble."

"How do you make that out?"

"Very easily. It is what has brought me to see you now. Listen—."

And then I did my best to explain the dangers of his position, and the folly of persisting in his present course of discontent and eccentricity.

"If you do not mind," I concluded seriously, "you will be treated to a strong dose of Medicated Schlafstrank some of these days, and then where will you be?"

Poor Augustus! Oh! how frightened he was! We were in the public gardens, and he staggered to a seat before he could say a word. Then he gasped, "Oh, Lord! deliver me from this land of iniquity! Help me to get home to my poor old mother, and I'll never swear at her again! She shall have the tickets for her gold watch and chain which I pawned, and if they'll take me on in the shop again I'll promise to work honestly, and pay for that suit of clothes I got on tick. And, oh, Lord, I'll turn up every penny of the money I cleared in that thimble-rigging business on Leger day. And that money I owe to the hotel-keeper, who thought I was Lord Hastings. I'll pay every farthing of it. Oh, Lord! let me get out of this very soon, or its two to one bar one that old Molly Jones will never see her son again!"

Here was a revelation! I could scarcely credit my ears. But the very evident terror of the man before me had brought out such truths as are only wrung from such lips as his by dire emergency, and I involuntarily recoiled from too near contact with an avowed blackguard, imposter, and cheat.

He noticed my gesture of repulsion, and cried imploringly, "Oh, for Heaven's sake, don't leave me! Help me to get out of this mess."

"I do not see what further help I can afford you," I responded coldly. "Your fate depends upon your own conduct."

"Ah, but there's no knowing what might happen, no matter what I say or do," he protested. "I must clear out somehow. And listen. I really have a plan. The reason I made a row about getting my own clothes back was because there was a tiny paper packet in the left waistcoat pocket. I had it given me at that opium den I was in in Soho. The fellow

ELIZABETH BURGOYNE CORBETT

that gave it me told me that it was a very wonderful sort of snuff, that would bring even funnier things to pass than Hasheesh could. I only remembered it the other day, and I thought it might perhaps help me to get home again. But it looks so queer that I am rather frightened of it. It might be poison, you know, and I thought I would see what you thought about it, before trusting myself to snuff any of it."

As he spoke he handed me the little paper parcel he had mentioned, and I examined it somewhat curiously. It certainly was uninviting, having a black and slimy appearance not at all pleasant to the eye. Still, it might smell much nicer than it looked, and as I fancied that I caught a faint, subtle aroma, I held the stuff to my nose, drew in a most delightful perfume, and—awoke in my own study, surrounded by nineteenth century magazines and newspapers, and shivering all over; for I had let the fire go out during my long nap.

A Note About the Author

Elizabeth Burgoyne Corbett (1846–1930) was an English novelist, journalist, and feminist. In addition to her work for the *Newcastle Daily Chronicle*, Corbett was a popular adventure and detective writer whose work appeared in some of the Victorian era's leading magazines and periodicals. In response to Mrs. Humphrey Ward's "An Appeal Against Female Suffrage," published in *The Nineteenth Century* in 1889, Corbett wrote *New Amazonia: A Foretaste of the Future* (1889), a feminist utopian novel set in a futuristic Ireland. Despite publishing a dozen novels and two collections of short fiction, Corbett—who was once described by *Hearth and Home* as a master of the detective novel alongside Arthur Conan Doyle—remains largely unheard of by scholars and readers today.

A Note from the Publisher

Spanning many genres, from non-fiction essays to literature classics to children's books and lyric poetry, Mint Edition books showcase the master works of our time in a modern new package. The text is freshly typeset, is clean and easy to read, and features a new note about the author in each volume. Many books also include exclusive new introductory material. Every book boasts a striking new cover, which makes it as appropriate for collecting as it is for gift giving. Mint Edition books are only printed when a reader orders them, so natural resources are not wasted. We're proud that our books are never manufactured in excess and exist only in the exact quantity they need to be read and enjoyed.

Discover more of your favorite classics with Bookfinity™.

- Track your reading with custom book lists.
- Get great book recommendations for your personalized Reader Type.
- Add reviews for your favorite books.
- AND MUCH MORE!

Visit **bookfinity.com** and take the fun Reader Type quiz to get started.

Enjoy our classic and modern companion pairings!

Printed in the USA
CPSIA information can be obtained
at www.ICGtesting.com
JSHW080001150824
68134JS00021B/2211